T0244973

DIVERSITY QUOTA

DIVERSITY QUOTA

Ranjan Adiga

THE UNIVERSITY OF WISCONSIN PRESS

Publication of this book has been made possible, in part,
through support from the Brittingham Trust.

The University of Wisconsin Press
728 State Street, Suite 443
Madison, Wisconsin 53706
uwpress.wisc.edu

Printed in the United States of America
This book may be available in a digital edition.

Library of Congress Cataloging-in-Publication Data

Names: Adiga, Ranjan, author.
Title: Diversity quota / Ranjan Adiga.
Description: Madison, Wisconsin : The University of Wisconsin Press, 2024.
Identifiers: LCCN 2024013179 | ISBN 9780299348441 (paperback)
Subjects: LCSH: Nepali people—Fiction. | LCGFT: Short stories. | Fiction.
Classification: LCC PR9570.N43 A35 2024 | DDC 823/.92—dc23/eng/20240405
LC record available at https://lccn.loc.gov/2024013179

Versions of stories in this collection were originally published in the
following journals: "High Heels" in La.Lit, 2024; "Spicy Kitchen" as
"Bombay Curry Kitchen" in Belmont Review, 2019; "Dry Blood" in
Packingtown Review, 2019; "Haircut and Massage" as "Haircut" in Story
Quarterly, 2009; "Kali" as "Pinky" in South Asian Review, 2009.

For Ma, Buwa, and Tenzing

Contents

DIVERSITY QUOTA

Denver

"Why can't we buy pinot noir from Walmart?" Sameer says as he stacks dinner plates in the dishwasher.

Puja rolls her eyes. "They hate cheap wine," she says.

"You should have baked a cake or something."

"The Nepali man speaks," Puja mumbles. "I was waiting for this."

Sameer doesn't want to prod. In Nepal their arguments would erupt into a fight, after which came the hard part, as if they had left behind a barrage of destruction and they had to dig through the rubble with their bare hands, trying to find something to hold on to. In America, the arguments dissipate into thin air, leaving residue in the walls and on their bed.

"Let's not spoil the mood right before we leave," Puja says.

They've been invited to an NFL watch party, hosted by the wealthy Sharmas. The theme is Broncos Barbecue, meaning everyone must wear their beloved team's jersey, which Puja has bought, without asking him, for forty dollars a piece on eBay.

On the way to the liquor store, they roll down the windows of their Toyota Corolla. The AC has stopped working again and the September air offers no reprieve. Sameer notices sweat drops on Puja's long legs that are on display beneath ripped shorts. Seeing her bare legs in public turns him on, a feeling that mingles with a mild irritation. They pick up a Napa Valley chardonnay, thirty dollars, not including tax.

Back in the car, Puja puts on her sunglasses and looks out the window without saying a word for the rest of the ride.

Just as they reach the Sharma house, Sameer takes her hand in his and says, "You regret marrying me, don't you?"

They sit quietly for a while.

"Make-up kiss?" she asks.

The kiss feels strained, a veiled attempt to reassure each other that they'd done the right thing by moving to America at a time when the arranged marriage had already borne some scars.

"I just wish you'd be a little open-minded sometimes," she says.

"What does open-minded have to do with buying alcohol?"

"I know you don't like me wearing shorts. You're being moody."

"*I'm* being moody?"

After she leaves the car, Sameer parks by the intersection, away from the BMWs and Teslas. The hosts, Raj and Maya Sharma, have plum jobs in IT, as do most of their guests. Sameer works at Walmart, Puja in an NGO for refugees. They can hardly afford to spend two hundred dollars—twenty-five thousand rupees—on these stupid parties thrown by wealthy Nepalis every month, but Puja insists. "Not showing up could cost us a favor," she says.

Sameer sits in the driver's seat and lights a cigarette. The houses that screen themselves behind walls look like houses where people never shout or fry their food. A cat stares at him from a balcony. In Nepal, Sameer had only seen stray cats cowering behind trash cans in narrow alleys. In America, he has realized it's not an animal you can smile at.

"You didn't have to!" Maya Sharma says in English, alluding to the wine. Her hair is dyed purple at the edges. Without leaving his shoes by the door, as would be the norm in a Nepali house, Sameer follows her through the foyer, brightly lit with a crystal chandelier. The spiral staircase is also lit with strips of mellow light.

"So, how's it going?" Maya says.

"Not bad, how are you?" Sameer responds in Nepali.

"Nicely buzzed," she says with a wink.

Sameer will never fully understand this person, her acquired but irrefutable Americanness. In the living room, Puja is standing with a glass of wine among women who talk brightly as they nibble on cheese and olives. An elderly woman, probably someone's mother visiting from Nepal, sits alone in a corner, her oversize Broncos jersey a mismatch with her sari.

Raj, the man of the house, is in charge of the grill in the backyard. Prosperity gives Americans the confidence to look casual, a trait Raj seems to have picked up with ease, considering the hole in his apron.

"Bro!" he shouts when he sees Sameer.

The game is live on a projector screen hooked on a stand under an awning. Men in their thirties sit around drinking beer. The charred smell of animal blood hangs over them.

"Still working the graveyard shift?" Raj asks, turning over a lamb patty.

"We do what we have to," Sameer says. He has sent his CV to multiple banks, even landed a phone interview without success.

A glass of whiskey in one hand, Raj reveals the superiority of a man confident of hosting a party in shorts and flip-flops. A white Labrador sits nearby, chewing on a fake bone.

"Remind me. Are you on H-1B?" Raj asks. He takes out a snuff box from his pocket and puts a dose of khaini, the cheap moist tobacco, behind his lower lip. The tobacco's stinging smell is like an invasion.

"DV," Sameer says and notices Raj's smirk.

Sameer and Puja had applied for the lottery visa on the off chance that they might win, to end up as one of fifty thousand winners from around the world. The news had been met with such jubilation, they had to throw a small party for all their neighbors in Kathmandu, some of whom brought gifts and CVs.

"Trump wanted to scrap DVs," Raj says, wiping his tobacco-stained finger on his apron. "I didn't always agree with the man, but he was right about immigration. Folks who come to this country on a lottery visa don't know what they're getting into. It's like letting in illegals legally. We had to slog it out the hard way through college."

When Sameer doesn't respond, Raj says, "I'm not talking about you guys. I mean the Bangladeshis, Afghanis. Those dog-headed Muslims."

Sameer holds back, knowing Puja wouldn't have let that slide. She would've given Raj an earful about discrimination. Why then does she insist on coming to these parties? "You can't hide from the truth," she says. "It's called networking."

Raj is still talking. He says he's impressed that Puja applied for a job at Goldman Sachs. Puja has never mentioned anything to Sameer about Goldman Sachs. But Raj goes on. He talks about a charity he is setting up to help child education in Nepal. He says he loves Nepal, but the country is like a chicken coop whose wires are falling apart. He doesn't stop rambling, pausing occasionally to spit into a flowerpot by the grill. As if his eye has never left the screen, he then twists his hip in a slow grind. "Yeah baby! Yeah baby!" he says when there's a touchdown. Other men, too, get up from their chairs—cheering, yelling. One man throws a beer-filled cup in the air.

A slow strain of anger forms inside Sameer like a taut wire. He feels stupid, wearing a jersey with the name Miller printed on it. He doesn't understand American football, and he can't shake off what Raj said about Puja and Goldman Sachs. Did he make that up, or did Puja tell everyone but her own husband?

Puja has a master's in economics from Kathmandu University, and because Sameer worked in a bank, she sends him links to articles about income inequality or health care spending, which he attempts to show interest in for the sake of spousal duty. She likes to teach him about stocks and trading in America, but the things *he* strives for—a midlevel bank job, a decent apartment, weekend trips to Costco—seem uninteresting to her. Even during those rare moments when they're in the apartment together, Puja sets an hour aside to read, an hour that stretches in front of him like a lifetime.

The time leading up to the wedding hadn't fully allowed them the chance to reveal oneself to the other. At the broker's house, a few months before the wedding, Sameer, who had never been with a girl, became infatuated. Puja was young, modern, and made eye contact. Her bra straps showed from underneath her cardigan, indicating a touch of carelessness that Sameer found sexy. She spoke for half an hour about her favorite author, Toni Morrison. That night Sameer googled Toni Morrison and was daunted by how complex the writing was. He also looked at Puja's profile on Instagram. She had volunteered at an animal shelter, trekked to Annapurna base camp, things he never dreamt of doing. Walking alongside her a few days later, as their shadows leaned in toward each other, Sameer had held her hand and said, "I think I'm ready for you." They were even considered an auspicious match by distant relatives who spoke highly of each other's families.

Soon after the wedding, Puja began guiding him during sex. Sameer found out that she was not a virgin. "You never asked," she said when he confronted her. She'd been in a relationship once, a long time ago, she said. Sameer became self-conscious of his own virginity. He had fantasized for years about the nights when he and his bride would explore the unaccustomed touch of desire together, little expecting the wife to be the one to initiate sex all the time. He felt it was a betrayal of sorts, and it changed the air around him. He concluded that this was the reason why Puja remained unmarried until twenty-seven. Nepali men would be curious about the women they were marrying, and Puja's lack of virginity, which she would have been honest about, would damage her prospects. Sameer hadn't wanted to pry too much into her life. Though he liked the idea of being with a progressive woman, he had simply refused to entertain the thought that Puja may have been in an intimate relationship before. Nepali women weren't supposed to cross that line.

"Why did you marry me? What did you really see in me?" Sameer had asked her.

A few months into the marriage, Sameer began spending long hours at the bank, preferring to go out for coffee with his friend Prakash, who spoke contently about marrying a woman who had grown up with the right values. "These so-called westernized girls are only good to flirt with," Prakash said. Sameer had discussed his wife's lack of virginity with Prakash, and this guilt consumed him. But he gradually found himself wondering if Prakash was right. Sameer did believe that women should have the same rights as men, but Puja's bold way of speaking her mind and arguing with him was like a sudden shock. He thought he was marrying someone who was smart but humble, intelligent but grounded, equally at ease driving a car as she was kneeling at a temple. When Puja told them she was an atheist, Sameer's mother had turned

away in embarrassment. Sameer knows he has been misled by his sim-
plicity. That's the word Puja uses to describe him—simple.

"I like you because you're a simple, honest guy," she says. Sameer
now finds himself unfamiliar with the smallest aspects of his wife's body,
because her self-assuredness keeps her slightly out of his grasp. When
Puja suggested moving abroad to start a new life together, Sameer acqui-
esced, despite his decent-paying job at Everest Bank, in the hope that
the change would be good, that they would still discover in one another
the companion that each longed for.

Wishing he was back in his apartment taking a nap on this cherished
Sunday, Sameer, who doesn't drink alcohol, slips in and out of small
groups—men in their loafers, pleasantly drunk, segregated from their
wives. He wanders beyond a latched fence door. A swimming pool
glimmers in the shape of an infinity sign, and the glass-wrapped house
of the Sharmas, perched on a hill near Cherry Creek, looks straight out
of a magazine cover. Sameer estimates the price to be at least a hundred
million rupees. In Nepal it would be the most expensive house, barring,
perhaps, the ex-king's palace.

Later, Sameer stands next to the old lady, in the corner of the living
room, watching Puja. A Bollywood song is booming over the walls and
the women are dancing in a circle. Barefoot, Puja looks vulnerable, sexy.
She sways her hips, moves her arms up her body as if she were taking
off her shirt. Sameer feels an erection, a gush of blood mixed with long-
ing and fear. This is a different Puja, quite a different woman from the
one at his apartment who is engrossed in her laptop when she isn't doing
a chore. Sameer wonders how he'll feel if he sees a man staring at his
wife. Jealous? Angry? Proud? Will he confront the man? Will he enjoy
watching the man watch his wife? He has played such scenarios endlessly in his mind but never reached the second act, because he becomes
sensitive and morose for thinking such thoughts.

When Puja sees him, she pulls him into the circle. The women cheer
them on. Sameer's legs refuse to budge as Puja bends her knees and
lets her body sway before his. He feels self-conscious about his crisply

ironed cotton pants, his fake Rolex, his hair glistening with coconut oil, neatly parted to one side. He tries to match her moves, but he is left feeling cold. He walks away, abruptly, but not before catching a glint of disappointment in Puja's eyes.

In the guest room by the foyer, large curtainless windows look out over the hills. Handwoven Tibetan carpets are thrown over the floorboards and a framed painting of Taleju, the ancient bell hanging between two pillars, adorns the wall. Sameer lies on the bed. Somewhere upstairs, kids run around creating thuds on the ceiling, and the laughter from the living room rises and falls.

He opens a window and lights a cigarette. That's how he bonded with Prakash, over cigarettes and coffee, talking about all the Nepali actresses they wanted to screw. Prakash says loving a wife is about control and Puja says love is about letting go. Puja had once asked him if he would be able to cope if she went alone to a different state for work or to attend university. Not knowing how to respond, Sameer had punched the wall, quickly regretting it, and pleading not to do it again, although she had refused to pack lunch for him that whole week. He didn't mind making the omelet sandwich as much as conceding, yet again, that she had been right. She'd told him he should have married a wife who had been groomed to cling like a vine, first to her father, then her husband. Looking across the manicured hedge at the silent street now, Sameer wonders if he is indeed a simple man who has never been put to the test about his values or has any real understanding of what those values even are. He had flirted with the idea of a modern woman because she seemed so far removed from his barely educated, conservative mother who forced him to go to temples, who still uses pronouns to address her husband. On the phone from Nepal, when his mother says that Prakash has chosen well, implying that her son is naive, Sameer defends Puja. "I don't want to hear another word about my wife," he says. What he wanted was that sweet spot in the middle, finding himself instead suspended between two worlds.

When he hears a knock, Sameer tosses the cigarette and closes the window.

"Puja needs you," Maya says, poking her head.

Sameer finds Puja slumped over the carpet, one hand tightly gripping an armchair. Her jersey is covered in vomit, and she isn't moving.

"I think she mixed her drinks," Maya says. She hands Sameer a plastic bag with a roll of paper towel and Clorox.

The smell is overpowering, causing everyone to speak in feigned normal voices.

"I feel terrible," Puja says when she sees him, and discharges a dry, guttural belch. She asks for a glass of water.

Sameer feels a flash of superiority. He kneels beside his wife and wipes the vomit from her face. "This is so embarrassing," he says.

The women pretend to look away, but Sameer is surprised to find the old lady standing behind him.

"Minced ginger with lime juice," the woman says abruptly.

"Thanks." Sameer takes the glass from her. The drink makes Puja grimace, but the woman insists.

"Ama, I'll take care of it," Sameer says. He removes the streaks of vomit stuck in his wife's hair and helps her to the bathroom, her arm around his neck, the woman a few steps behind.

"It's fine, ama," Sameer says.

He sits Puja down on the toilet and changes her into a clean T-shirt and pajamas that Maya had given him. He cleans her face again with a wet paper towel, tsk-tsking when he notices a fleck stuck in her neck. "How much did you drink, anyway?" he asks without expecting a response. When they emerge from the bathroom, the old woman is standing with some cloves.

"Make her chew these. She'll feel better."

"Give us some privacy, will you? This is America," Sameer yells at her. It comes out like an uncontrollable itch. The woman leaves, waving them off with her palm.

After helping Puja to bed in the guest room, Sameer goes back and scrapes off every particle stuck in tiny sprouts of yarn. He sprays a generous amount of Clorox. He does the best he can, but the blotch on the sofa won't scrub off.

"Don't use that chemical on the sofa!" Maya says, startling him. "I'll call the cleaner tomorrow."

She opens the windows to air out the smell. The chatter and music resume.

"Why didn't you go to the bathroom?" he asks Puja when they're alone.

"It happened so quickly."

"How much did you drink anyway? You never really drank in Nepal."

"You've made your point," she says. "I said sorry."

"No, you haven't," he says.

She reaches for his hand, locks her fingers into his.

"How was the networking?" he says.

She laughs. "Maya is actually a nice person. Unlike her boneheaded husband," she says, her voice slightly slurred.

"Remember when we couldn't afford a sofa and we'd sit on a couch at Costco?" he says, looking at the ceiling.

"We fell asleep once. They tapped our shoulders because you were snoring," she says with a chuckle. "Deep down you're a kind person and that's what I liked in you. A genuine person. Sameer Karki. Unpretentious. Hardworking. Hot. Are you Mr. Hot?"

"Let's see. Smart, daring, secretive," he says. "Making me find out about Goldman Sachs from other people."

"I haven't applied yet. Of course, I would tell you." She turns to face him, her breath a sweet-sour mixture of wine and vomit. "I only had a chat with Maya. About the corporate world," she says.

"You've always kept secrets from me," he says. "From day one."

"You're such an insecure man-child." She lets get of his hand.

"You know, you've never told me. How was the sex with your boyfriend?" he says.

"It was so great, I miss it every day," she says.

"Get it off your fucking chest."

"We did it everywhere. On the bed. On the floor. Even in the bathroom of his office when he called me at night from work."

Sameer's throat becomes dry.

There is a pause. "Why are you doing this?" Puja finally asks.

The question has been asked, answered, and can no longer be retracted. "I want to know," he says.

After another pause, she says, "It was never planned. We didn't know when to stop."

Sameer is excited like one might be when preparing for a mild shock. He has spent so much time thinking about it. How did the man's lips move across every part of his wife's body? Did his tongue brush against the dark circles around her nipples?

"And?" he asks.

"You really want to go there?"

"Tell me," he says, staring at the ceiling.

"There was this time in his SUV. We were in a busy parking lot in New Road. Tinted glass. I was on top of him . . ."

"And?" Sameer's heart is thumping against his chest.

"We were naked. He grabbed my ass."

Sameer is tempted to go farther, but Puja keeps quiet. She slides her hand underneath his underwear. He is hard. She strokes his penis. Sameer arches his neck back. His muscles tense and relax. She takes him in her mouth.

"Did he fuck you like an animal?" he asks, his voice trembling.

Minutes later, he is inside her.

All his frustration and anger coagulate in his groin, and the bed creaks as their bodies pulse and vibrate.

"We had sex in a swimming pool," she says. Sameer feels effervescent bubbles in his thighs like he's never felt before.

The smoke detector goes off. Someone knocks.

"What's going on?" Puja says, sitting up in bed, covering herself with the sheet.

From the other side of the door, Maya says, "Can I come in? I need to take out the battery."

"No!" says Sameer.

They wait. He gets up, wrapped in a sheet, and presses his ear against the door.

"Is she there?" Puja whispers.

"I don't think so," he says and locks the door.

The machine, thankfully, stops chirping.

They breathe in the lingering silence, not knowing how to face each other.

"He was awful," Puja says. "Dominating. Cheated on me."

She pulls him next to her, but the mood is gone, so they end up masturbating on their own. When she cries on her side of the bed, Sameer rubs her bare shoulder, not knowing, yet knowing exactly why she's crying. She had expected him to be an open slate but can't extricate him from the entangled beliefs he comes with, just as he has tied himself to a person he has little in common with. For months afterward, however, he will ask, reluctantly at first, then openly, and she will describe, without leaving out any detail, like that time when her ex-lover took her from behind in the Yak & Yeti swimming pool while she held on to the ladder as tourists snoozed in pool chairs. Sameer gets so turned on, they make love until they can't move, and Puja will come up with a different story each time, hurling them into a new direction they must learn to navigate. The anticipation of fear arouses something inside Sameer, the fear that he might not measure up, mixed with the excitement of jealousy, and Puja grasps on to this, because the pleasure is intense, and that seems tenuously enough to hold on to.

After she nods off, breathing with her mouth open, her dark eye circles transparent underneath the makeup, Sameer puts on his clothes and goes out of the room, hungry.

He bumps into Maya in the foyer.

"You guys should come more often. In this country, we're fingers in a fist," she says, the last part in Nepali, and Sameer wonders if she's tipsy.

"I'm so sorry, again," he says.

"Apparently, she puked after two glasses of wine? Cute," Maya says.

∾

Sameer is grateful to find a spread of dal, rice, and vegetables in the backyard. By now, everyone is at various levels of melancholy, clustered in their small groups, talking about politics or work problems. As he fills up two plates, one for Puja, Sameer notices the old woman, sitting on a chair under an oak tree, counting rosary beads. He sits next to her, a plate of rice and dal in one hand, and a plate covered with foil for Puja.

"How's your wife?" she asks.

"Resting," he says. "I didn't mean to yell at you earlier. I apologize."

They watch two squirrels chase each other on the edge of the yard fence.

"How far is the Nepali store from here? My daughter and son-in-law can take me in their car, but I don't want to bother them always. Is there a bus?" she says.

"There is an Indian store not too far away." He offers to give her a ride the next day and tells her about the bus route. He explains the direction, the different buses she needs to take. She could buy the RTD daily, weekly, or monthly pass and take the light rail, but make sure to get off on Akron and take the 42. Sameer knows that she won't remember any of that, but he still takes pleasure in explaining how things work in America.

Leech

When Ram looked in the mirror one morning, he saw a leech dangling from his nose. He screamed, more from shock than pain. In fact, there was no pain even as the leech crawled back inside his nostril.

"I'm not joking, and I have that job interview today," he told Juneli on the phone. She was busy in a client meeting.

"I'll see what I can do," she said.

A classmate from his college, Juneli came from a wealthy Kathmandu family. It mattered to Ram that she was kind to him at a time when migrants were blamed for the ills in the city, especially a darker-skinned Madhesi like him. Ram had grown up in the flatlands near India. With a whiff of derision, he was constantly asked if he was Indian, and his accent had become a butt of jokes at work.

"I love this about you," Juneli said when she showed up later.

It was a shoe rack made from used cardboard. Ram liked tinkering with odds and ends, an old habit that had acquired a new significance since Juneli started coming to his apartment. Her favorite was a mini fan built from plastic spoons and wires hooked up to a DC motor. It made a whirring sound, though not so much as paper stirred.

When Ram was fired, it was Juneli he had turned to. He had no idea Mountain Wonders, the travel agency he worked for, was involved in a racket. The agency came under scrutiny after some amateur European trekkers died during an expedition on Everest, and the media reported that Mountain Wonders had been selling illegal climbing permits without conducting background checks. Under normal circumstances, the Nepali government would have turned a blind eye, but the pressure from European embassies meant something had to be done. A handful of agencies were raided, under-the-table deals struck, and Ram was among a group of junior accountants who were made scapegoats. Of course, Ram knew he was fired because he was a migrant without family connections in a city easily swayed by influence. Suddenly out of work and cash-strapped, he was glad when Juneli negotiated a job interview. She knew someone who knew someone who was hiring an assistant in an engineering firm.

She used the light in her phone to peek inside Ram's nose. The leech appeared briefly, before slipping back.

She gasped.

"It doesn't hurt," he said.

"Wouldn't your mother have a cure? Clarified butter? Turmeric paste? Something traditional? This could be poisonous," she said.

Ram's mother *did* have a homemade remedy for every ailment, but the crackle of wires over the long-distance call would add to everyone's anxiety. Juneli tried to look for a solution online, but the Wi-Fi was slow.

"I can't even afford a doctor," Ram said. Juneli knew, yet he found himself glancing at her, trying to catch an accidental sneer.

"Why don't you sell these useless books?"

Hardbound volumes on engineering and philosophy lined his bookshelf. Who would buy these obscure tomes he had taken from discarded boxes at the college library? There was even a 1956 edition of *Russian Engineering Marvels* written in Buryat, a Mongolian dialect.

"I have an attachment to them that I can't explain," he said.

"The nostalgic migrant," she said. She lay down in his bed, her head on his pillow. Her fair and flawless skin seemed hereditary, evidence of wealth.

"A man burned himself in protest. When will politicians learn that we can't be a real democracy without Madhesi inclusiveness?" Juneli said.

Her dark toenail polish added the glamor quotient in this meager room as did her Louis Vuitton purse, which Ram knew was not a Chinese knockoff because it had a code stitched on a tag. Ram had read about this authentication code and had looked for it one day when she was in the bathroom. When he opened her purse, he wasn't surprised to find a wad of cash and an expensive-looking perfume, but he was shocked to learn from a website that this purse cost at least fifty thousand rupees, more than what his two-month salary used to be. For a moment, he had been tempted to steal the money.

Ram sat on a plastic chair as Juneli complained about the state of politics, running her finger along the pattern on the bedsheet. Later, he would smell the sheet because the flowery perfume lingered long after she left. He often wondered about their relationship, and how difficult it had been to define it. She once came out of the bathroom in her house covered in nothing but a towel, exposing wet hair and shoulders. Ram wasn't sure if this was an invitation, or if such a display of comfort canceled out any possibility of romance. His visits to her palatial house had increased over the months, signaling a slight change of attitude in Seeta and Geeta, her teenage maids, who no longer smirked at his frayed backpack or socks that sagged from overuse. They even let Catty Perry climb on his lap.

"This is my friend from Janakpur," was how Juneli had introduced him to the overfed cat who stared at him so fiercely he had to turn his face away. Ram had considered stepping on the cat's tail on more than one occasion, just as he had considered tasting the Rémy Martin from the living room bar, discouraged only by the maids' instincts to read his mind. Juneli liked to stress that the maids went to school and read books in English. They recited a stanza from "Solitary Reaper" in unison when they first met Ram. They looked at him, and he at them, like they all knew he had narrowly escaped their fate.

"Hungry? I can fry some pakoras," Ram said. He liked whipping up Terai-style pakoras heavy on the onion for her. He had even started to store fresh vegetable batter in a water-filled pot in anticipation of her visits, and she showed her appreciation by licking her fingers, telling him what a great cook he was.

It was six months ago when Juneli had spoken up in his defense. Ram never said a word in class except this one time when he spoke in favor of more Madhesi representation in the parliament. His accent was so strong, people's ears perked up. He had to repeat himself for the benefit of their amusement. When a classmate questioned Madhesis' patriotism because of their ties to India, Juneli called that person's comments racist.

"Not racism if we're the same race," someone said.

"Fine. Prejudiced, bigoted—take your pick," Juneli shot back.

From a distance, Ram had been intrigued by Juneli, her unapologetic views, the cropped hair, nose ring, the tattoo of a raised fist on her arm. Later he would read the word *socialistfeminist* stitched into the contours of the clenched fingers. After class, she sat next to him in the canteen. "I hate entitled assholes," she said. She liked to casually drop words like asshole and fuck. They sounded cool in English. You needed a natural confidence to pull it off. She also told him she never had a Madhesi friend, and they spent that afternoon talking about their shared hatred for the ruling right-wing party. Ram had felt a sudden gush of love for the world that day.

∾

"Daydreaming?" she asked.

"No, of course not."

"I said I managed to sneak out for a while. The boss is on my case, so no time for your pakoras."

Ram was surprised by how comfortable she made herself in his flat, never complaining about the frequently dried-up taps or the noise from the street. She liked to make tea on his kerosene stove that ignited a sharp flame when you pushed the pump. The trick was to push rapidly. It was an acquired skill and Juneli had mastered it after several attempts.

"Did you know?" she asked, facing him, the length of her legs covering his bed. "Lord Indra was cursed with yonis that sprouted like mushrooms in his body. If an alien invades your body, it's god's way of telling you to stop thinking about sex."

Ram caught his reflection in the cupboard mirror blemished with spots; his wiry, dark-brown muscles a sharp contrast to her light skin. Placed by the bed, the mirror allowed him a view of her buttocks, perfectly bulging under the tight jeans.

"Didn't Freud say something about stress and sexual energy?" he asked, pivoting the conversation slightly. He couldn't imagine talking so frankly about sex with a girl. In his district, wall slogans about family planning were conveyed through intertwined flowers and two sprouting buds, underneath the words, *Us two, ours two.* When a trickle of warm blood dripped from his nose, Ram was rather relieved and remembered why he had called her in the first place.

"You need to go to a doctor," Juneli said. She called her office and told them she would come in a little late.

Ram wasn't comfortable borrowing money from her. They split costs at the college canteen, and he was careful to write down every expense in his notebook, returning what he owed no later than the third of each month. Friends in villages pretended to forgive small debts, but Juneli was frank about divvying up costs from day one, which he noticed after she paid for their tea, followed by, "How do you want to pay me back?" He had been shocked by her frankness. It was sundry expenses, coffee or momo, which she paid with her debit card. Precisely on the first of every month, a WhatsApp message pinged on his phone with a screenshot of the amount, down to decimal points. Once he had been late to pay, and she sent a text with four words that left him feeling cold—*Just a friendly reminder.*

Ram insisted on going to a cheaper Ayurvedic doctor, but Juneli dismissed it with a wave of her hand. "You can borrow the money from me. Why are you being so stubborn?" she retorted. Twenty minutes later, though, they were standing next to a signboard dangling from an electric pole. We Purify Bad Blood, it pledged with an arrow pointing to a disheveled clinic.

A curtain hung in the middle of the room to separate the dispensary from the kitchen. Baidya Ba's thick glasses were held together with black tape. He sat behind a cabinet with potions in colorful bottles.

They waited for the leech in silence.

"It's no more poisonous than a mosquito," Baidya Ba said in an assured tone, anticipating his patient's distress. He pushed a curtain back and stepped into the other side of the shop, and Ram caught a glance of a woman cutting vegetables on a plate. The man returned with a pair of tweezers and a bowl of water. He asked Ram to tip his head back, and without warning, tossed a handful of water inside the nostrils. The leech came out and regarded them quizzically.

"Ah! Leeches cling to the body heat of people who smell," the old man said.

"Say that again?" Juneli said.

Still feeling the sting in his nose, Ram poked her shoulder with his elbow. He could see a strain of anger already curling around the edge of her lips. "Let it go," he whispered. The man was unable to tame the leech with his tweezers. It bobbed its head like a cobra before slipping back inside, so he gave Ram a bottle of eucalyptus oil.

"Rub this on your nose. It'll stop the bleeding and the leech will fall off on its own. Five hundred rupees," the man said, holding out his palm for the money.

Ram looked at Juneli in disbelief. He checked every pocket hoping a magic stash would appear. Finally, Juneli took out cash from her purse and shoved it into the man's hand.

"I'll pay you back as soon as I can," Ram said.

As they walked toward her scooty, Juneli said, "Fucking racist. Madhesis are Nepali too. I mean, you guys are people too."

"Touch my hand. I'm a real human." Ram smiled.

"You know what I mean."

"We have to finish *The Road to Serfdom* for class this evening. Just reminding you. That professor asks questions," he said.

"How much money do you send your parents every month, by the way? I've always wondered. Do they know you were fired?"

After a brief pause, Ram said, "I send them what I can," silently annoyed by the abrupt question. Juneli had this way of asking startlingly direct questions that came out of nowhere. She had caused him great embarrassment this one time when she introduced him to one of her friends, supposedly the son of an industrialist, and asked in front of the stranger, "What do your parents do? You've never told me how poor they actually are." When Ram said they were farmers, she asked if they were tenant farmers and went on about the problem of farmer suicides in South Asia, while he stood awkwardly and her friend listened in apathetic silence. Later she asked him if she had been intrusive when he told her he didn't like talking about his family that way.

"You didn't like that question, right?" she now said as they approached her scooty.

"I prefer not to talk about my family," he said.

They walked quietly for a while, then she punched his shoulder in a friendly way.

"I appreciate you so much, Ram Mishra," she said, and contrary to his inherent pessimism, Ram had learned to ignore a streak of insensitivity concealed under her thick layer of warmth.

The scooty's headlights were like a horse's eyes; mirrors perched up like ears. Juneli maneuvered between humans and cars through the dense traffic, cooking up a story here and a story there, usually about being late to a hospital, and though the drivers knew she was lying, they let her sneak past tight spaces. If Ram drove, which he did on occasion, he loved the rush of air against his neck, and wondered if Juneli might put her arms around his waist.

When she dropped him off, he asked, "Do I smell? It's the hair oil, isn't it?"

She laughed. "Your hair smells of coconut oil. And fennel seeds. It's sexy," she said, a flash of tease in her eyes. "Call me," she said, before speeding off to work.

Ram stood there for a while with a smile on his face. Later, in his room, he rubbed his nostril with the eucalyptus oil, which caused a mild irritation before the muscle tissues relaxed. Ram wrote down five hundred in his notebook, next to a litany of expenses.

Strange one, Juneli. The daughter of rich lawyers, her anger against oppression seemed exaggerated sometimes—as if she were making up for a lack of experience, or simply acting out to prove something to him. She worked as a paid intern in the nation's largest advertising agency, "as an experiment," and in college, she explored courses like Festivals in

Film, which had no bearing on her career. He wondered if she caught sight of him when his eyes sometimes landed on her breasts, or what her reaction might be if she found out that he kissed his pillow after she left, not just a light peck, but a deep kiss that left a wet smudge on the cloth. He was smiling at this idiocy when he remembered he had a leech inside his nose and a job interview in a few hours.

The Wi-Fi was easier to hack when the landlords were at lunch. Ram had purchased an old laptop from them. He wiped it several times a day and locked it in his cupboard when he wasn't using it. He had lived long enough to know that disaster was close at hand and if something happened to his laptop, he would lose his fight with the world.

"Inflation Creates Chaos in Kathmandu," screamed a news headline. The scapegoating of migrants was never overt, but you saw it if you knew how and where to look, like this piece that attributed a questionable statistic about mass migration to an unnamed source. In the comment section, Ram wrote, "If all the migrants left, Kathmandu's economy would crash in seconds." He typed comments using his real name. It gave him a visceral excitement to argue freely online.

He could never forget that day. Late afternoon. The sun had such a glare, it was impossible to look up at the sky. Eight-year-old Ram was carrying rotis, kept warm in a piece of cloth, meant for his parents who were working in the field. When he finally reached a clearing, walled on all sides by sugarcane plants, Ram saw his mother pointing a scythe at the drunk landlord who was waiting to pounce on her. The stack of roti fell to the ground, and without a thought, Ram hurled a stone at the man. It struck him on the nose. The bleeding man howled like an animal. The same man Ram had been taught to wave at by his father, who was obliviously hacking into cane sticks on the other side of the field. Their meager savings were stolen after the incident. The bank sided with the landlords, while Ram's family struggled for months, farmhands with no work or money, living on the generosity of relatives, until they moved from place to place, finally settling in a village where the rumors could no longer reach them. His ageing mother and father dug their heels in paddy fields when work was available. Ram, the oldest of three, became a resolute student, eventually winning a pre-engineering scholarship in a college in Kathmandu. He knew a master's degree, which he was determined to pursue, would create a stir in his village.

Two hours later, Ram was done preparing notes for the interview when his thoughts strayed back to the leech, still snuggled inside his nose. The scandal would be too much if it wiggled out during the interview. He called Juneli.

"Can you please give me a ride to a real doctor?"

She agreed but looked distracted when she came.

"There's a YouTube video about this—what should we call it, an infection? A plague? We must go to a dermatologist," she said.

"I don't want to borrow more money from you."

"Then sell something for fuck's sake," she said in English.

Ram held on to his bicycle precariously balanced between them, and off they went on her scooty, along an unpaved road next to a highway built with Chinese money. Glaring billboards along the highway carried advertisements promising silky, shiny hair. Ram remembered that his family shared a single towel when he was a child. His mother would rub his wet hair with the thin cotton fabric that she had just wiped herself with, quickly and roughly, before she did the same to his younger brother and sister, so that they didn't have to stand naked and exposed at the communal tap. His mother had never experienced the luxury of a proper bath in the nude as an adult, covered as she was with a petticoat from her breast to her knees while strange men brushing their teeth stared at her, hoping for a slip. On one occasion, Ram had held on to the towel aggressively, like a prized possession he didn't want to let go. After prying it away from him, his mother had slapped him, and he had cried saying, "I don't have anything."

They reached a dry expanse where clumps of weed grew out of old cars piled up like tin boxes. A mechanic appeared from behind a car stripped to its bones. His shirt pocket bristled with an assortment of pliers. He turned Ram's bicycle upside down, checked the spokes, chain, brakes. Ram had hooked up a small box on the handlebar as a placeholder for his phone so that he wouldn't miss a text from Juneli. The bike was sold for a fraction of what Ram had paid for it, barely enough for a doctor's fee.

Above the clamor of sputtering engines, welding machines, hammer on metal, Ram told Juneli that he might have to borrow some money from her after all.

"I get so tired of your secrets. Why didn't you just borrow the whole amount from me in the first place? I'm trying to help," she said.

The skin around Ram's mouth became taut. On the ride to the clinic, they quietly nursed their own miseries.

Lucky to get an appointment on the same day, Ram closed his fatigued eyes in the air-conditioned waiting room. He dreamt that his intestine had turned into a giant leech throbbing with life. He was startled awake from the dream, surprised to find Juneli asleep, her head on his shoulder. Her mouth was open as if she were waiting for a bite to eat. The purse was on her lap. Ram's hand reached for it without thinking. His brain was no longer working within his body. A sudden shiver ran down his neck. "She won't notice," he whispered to himself. He took out three thousand rupees and shoved the notes into his pocket. When his name was called, he woke her up with a gentle push.

The doctor's walls were filled with family photos that linked him to a life of tennis courts and beaches. He leaned back in his leather chair, folding his clean hands. He peered into Ram's face as if he was in search of a redeeming grace. "Where are you from?" he asked.

"Near Janakpur, sir."

The doctor tapped Ram's nose with a finger and the leech's head came into view.

"Did you swim in a river recently?" the doctor asked.

Indeed. A few days ago, when Ram had gone to Malekhu for a class project, he'd dunked his head under a waterfall that flowed like a tiny stream, accumulating minerals from rocks, forming a natural spout on a cliff's edge. The crystal-clear water had given him the kind of joy he got when swimming in a clean river.

"Village water is full of leeches. One of them must have dived into your nose." The doctor prescribed diethyltoluamide cream and oxymetazoline tablets. For such a clean man, his handwriting was sloppy. "Buy these from the pharmacy below. Rub number one on your nose twice daily. Take number two three times a day."

"Sir, I have a job interview today. Could there possibly be a quicker fix?"

The doctor adjusted the room temperature with a remote control.

"What about a discount? Does your fancy clinic lack total empathy for the financially disadvantaged, which is approximately eighty-five percent of the country?" Juneli asked.

The doctor could perhaps tell that she was privileged from her purse, her demeanor.

He handed her a brochure. "We're building schools in several districts, with free medical care." He held up a picture of village girls next to the words "USAID, donor money channeled through local hospitals and clinics." "You can go to the website to donate," he said, and added, "In fact, let me give this man a discount. Why not?"

"How much?" she asked.

"Twenty percent."

"Twenty-five? Please, Doctor saab. He's come all the way from Janakpur."

"Is that so?" The doctor scribbled something on the prescription and continued talking to her.

Ram got up and left without the discounted prescription. He walked down the long corridor, hungry for air. He felt guilty and angry. A coldness settled on his bones. He had never stolen anything. Juneli *would* find out and it wouldn't be a happy ending. He paid the full consultation fee at the reception. Juneli, who had caught up with him, pretended to look at her phone the whole time. He kept walking ahead of her, and at the pharmacy, he bought a pair of tweezers but couldn't afford the medicine unless he used the stolen money, which she would ask him about. He wished she hadn't followed him.

"You're not taking advantage of the discount? When have you ever gotten a discount at a clinic?" she asked.

"Can we not talk about it?" Ram said.

Juneli gave him the silent treatment during the ride to his place. A mixture of guilt and fear burrowed into him. The coldness he had felt now burned like heat in his body. He couldn't concentrate on anything but the purse, hanging on a strap, draped over her shoulder. It bounced against her thigh on the bumpy road.

When they reached his apartment, he said, "The doctor's conde-
scension was startling. Like I am everyone's sympathy project."

"Sometimes you must play the game to beat the system. I wouldn't
ask for a discount for myself, but you needed it."

When nothing came out of his mouth, but a hollow breath of air,
Juneli shook her head.

∽

Ram propped his head against the bedpost as Juneli bent over him.

She gently guided the tweezers inside the nose.

"Don't move," she said in a soft voice, as if any unwanted gesture
would break her concentration. He noticed the split between her breasts
behind the unhooked buttons. Her perfume smelled faint, and a dapple
of freckles looked sexy against her light skin.

"I have a project deadline at five. My boss keeps texting me. I've
taken one day off this whole year, and he still treats me like he'll cut me
loose if I so much as blink at the wrong time," she said.

"He'll never fire you. Your boss will probably get fired before he fires
you. All your mom has to do is make a phone call."

She sat up. "Say again?"

"That came out wrong," he lied.

"Try again. Speak a full paragraph for once."

"You know what my boss called me before he fired me?" Ram said.
"Mr. Cunning, like he meant it as a compliment. You know the stereotype, Madhesis are shifty, untrustworthy. He said, 'You people . . . I have
no doubt you'll find a job somewhere.'"

She looked like she was struggling with anguish. Finally, she said, "As
a financially disadvantaged minority, you have the right to claim a discount in a clinic that is catered to the rich in a country where the poor
die of medical bills. That is, if their disease doesn't kill them first. But
you're so busy feeling sorry for yourself that you can't see the bigger
picture."

She sat in the middle of the bed. Her cheeks were red with the blood
that had rushed to them. "The wall of silence that you hide your thoughts

behind. What are you thinking of when I catch you staring at me?" she asked.

Ram had not been trained like her—to turn thoughts into words that spat out of a mouth in perfectly formed meanings. His mouth became dry.

"I'm supposed to be at work, and you just assume, maybe because I'm a girl, that I should just tag along. And I do. Why? Because I've never met someone so desperate," she said.

He wondered if she had an inbred vanity that she hid carefully, but it made quite an appearance when she got prickly.

"I dragged you into my mess," he finally said.

"Let's get this over with," she said, shaking her head. A careful effort later, she clenched the leech.

"Keep calm," she said quietly.

The first inch of the leech came out without a struggle, but then it became stubborn and refused to be drawn out. Juneli kept persevering until it released its hold bit by bit. Finally, it was hanging on the tweezers, puffed up with Ram's blood.

"Freak. Do you know how much suffering you've caused?" Juneli screamed at the leech. Ram was laughing too, and he must have looked like a maniac, chuckling with a bloody nose.

Later he sent her a text—*Thank you. You've done a lot for me.*

She didn't reply.

~

When Juneli first caught sight of him at the college later that evening, she looked away quickly. But he approached her anyway.

"I didn't get the job," he said. He hadn't been able to concentrate during the interview. He had decided to come clean and return the money after class.

Juneli gave him an unexpected hug. If Ram had to recreate that moment he couldn't. It wasn't just that it was a full embrace, her arms around his shoulders, but in that quick moment he found his own arms around her as if they were hungry to absorb the sadness of the other.

"You should start looking at the classifieds," she said and pulled away from him.

For the next hour, the economics teacher droned on about micro-lending. When he thought about how Juneli might react when he told her about the money, the fear in Ram's belly turned into something like bubbles in a rancid swamp. Her rejection of him would be too final, irrevocable. He watched her taking notes or writing something. What-ever it was, she was jabbing at the keyboard with intent.

That image of his mother holding the scythe had jolted him awake in cold sweat from countless nightmares. She went about her life qui-etly after the incident, not a word spoken about what had happened. It was when she oiled her long hair every morning, the sharp bristles of her comb boring into every strand, that she seemed to gather into her-self all the threads of her life. You couldn't shatter her concentration with a hammer in those moments. Ram would stare at her in fascina-tion and fear, feelings that thawed only when his mother became her affectionate self at night when she hugged her children tightly, running her bony fingers through their hair as if she were trying to discern their dreams. Ram now stared at Juneli in the same way. He felt similarly awed by her, but there was something else about Juneli—a chasm, or at least a feeling of a chasm, that rose up from the earth and spread into the sky to keep them in their own separate worlds forever. It wasn't like his mother's silence that he could settle on, a silence that did not seem distant or cold. But alien. His mother was surrounded by a constella-tion of worlds he could never reach, but Ram knew in his heart that his mother would never reject him.

Juneli suggested a light snack after class. She offered to pay for Wai Wai and Coke, but Ram insisted. "You've done a lot for me. This is the least I can do," he said.

The evening sky was filled with the smell of approaching rain. They sat on top of milk crates outside a shop. Juneli turned on the headlight on her scooty. Instantly, a cluster of bugs nosedived into this source of light.

"We need to talk," she finally said. "I know you took money from my purse."

He had prepared for this moment, and yet, he felt an uneasiness in his heart. "I was about to return it," he said. "Trust me. I swear." He took out the cash from his wallet.

"Keep it," she said. "I'm not okay with what happened. You have a world within you that I don't have access into. The sad thing is, I thought I knew you, but I don't. I do not really know who you are."

He held her hand. The simple gesture made him nervous. She flinched.

"I'm disappointed. We can't meet anymore . . . at least for a while," she said.

"For a while?"

"I don't know if I'll ever feel comfortable seeing you. What made you steal my money? It's such a deep betrayal."

Ram didn't have an answer that could swiftly release the tension. "I'm sorry," was all that he could say. He meant it, though the banality made the apology sound disingenuous. When the rain came down in a light shower, it made him sadder than he had ever been.

Spicy Kitchen

"What's the capital of Burkina Faso?" I ask.

"Seriously?"

"You're African. You're supposed to know that."

"Africa is a continent. With fifty countries. At least," Ali says.

"I think I could tell you the name of every Asian capital. Try me."

He looks at his phone. "Kyrgyzstan."

"Bishkek."

"I hate you," he says.

At least Ali is not as bad as the Americans. I went on this road trip for a science project. When the teacher said, "Let's play name the capital," I had no idea she meant state capitals. They knew the capital of Maine but not Spain. I'm not even talking about an obscure country like Ghana, but Spain? I guess you can't expect much from a country that calls its baseball league championship the "World Series."

"Stop sulking. What's the score?" I ask. Ali is a Man U fan. I'm Chelsea through and through. The only world sport worth its salt—the glorious and graceful football. Yes, sir, I refuse to call it soccer.

Ali claims to be the biggest football fan who has actually never played a game. I never thought I'd meet a nerdy African. He wears a crisp shirt and perfectly ironed cotton pants, out of sync with the red headphones and Air Jordan sneakers. It's the look of a new immigrant, caught between modesty and swag. Ali is a refugee from Somalia who came to

Utah with his mother and sister several months ago, barely seventeen and already a survivor of war.

"If I had a work permit, I'd be working at Best Buy, not as a dishwasher," I say as we wait for the bus to take us to the restaurant. I'm from Nepal, and unlike Ali, I'm on a student visa. The Indian owners couldn't pass up the opportunity to hire me on the cheap—three dollars less than minimum wage, that's three dollars less than what Ali makes every hour. We clean, scrub, cook, wait, bus, and don't get a dime of the tips. I can't wrap my head around the fact that Ali isn't more ambitious. The guy was handed his work permit with resettlement funds as soon as the wheels touched the tarmac.

"I'm seventeen," Ali says. "You're twenty-one. There's a big difference."

"You know at what age kids start working in Nepal? Ten. They clean houses before they learn how to clean their own dicks. But we don't get foreign aid like you do because we're not called Africa."

"Let it go," he says.

We wait in silence, next to an endless highway that cuts across vast open fields where horses work themselves into shape and cows get fat. The mountains are so close you can see the cracks on their faces, and out of the wilderness rise the yellow arches of McDonald's, the only building for miles, lifting the spirits of every weary traveler driving to Las Vegas. This is a remote part of Cedar City, a tiny speck of American desert known as flyover country. The only other person at the bus stop is a White woman. She looks up from her phone every now and then to check for the bus.

"They said go where the mountains are, you'll feel less homesick. These mountains are just giant red rocks," I say.

"Best to be positive," Ali says.

"How did *you* guys end up here? I've never asked."

"Our agent said there are so many Somalis in Utah, someone is bound to be a distant cousin. He put an X over Utah on the American map. It looked like a treasure hunt. We were lucky to be chosen for the USA, but I'd never heard of Utah. I thought it's America, so it must have tall glass buildings everywhere."

"More like tall rocks and more rocks," I say half-jokingly because even in this land of farmers, I'm breathing American air. I pinch myself every day that I actually made it. But there's a catch. If I don't pay my remaining tuition balance at the end of this semester, I won't be allowed to register for classes next spring. If I don't register, I'll be out of status, meaning undocumented. Illegal. Extraterrestre, amigo. It's scary how quickly things can turn around.

"You should apply for an asylum visa," Ali says.

Someone in Nepal *could* forge papers claiming that I'm a political refugee, but my parents can't bribe the fixers and lawyers. The old Western Union receipts that I've saved in a shoebox are a reminder that they've done their part. They're middle-class Nepali who eagerly await news of progress: graduation, job, house, green card.

"About time," the woman says, rolling her eyes in a familiar way. In the eighty-seven-degree heat, the bus appears in the distance like a mirage.

"Thank god for public transportation," I say. My accent can leak out like a bad smell. It turns some people off, but she smiles cheerfully.

"Where are you guys from?" she asks.

"I go to SUU," I say.

"But where are you *really* from?"

"Nepal and Somalia."

"That's so cool!" she says, and we wait in the awkward silence for the bus to open its doors with a hiss.

It takes an hour to ride the ten miles to Spicy Kitchen. The few White people on the bus look poor and depressed, and the smell of unwashed clothes linger in the seat.

"About those college fees," Ali says, the shiny headphones emblazoned with the letter *b* hanging on his neck. "How *will* you pay?"

"Rob a gas station. Meet me downtown tonight."

Ali smiles. It's a polite way of thumbing your nose at someone. The dude has an apartment that the state pays for, while I'm allowed to work *only* on campus *only* for twenty hours a week, shelving books at the library every morning before class. How will that pay for my education? The college takes care of my meal plan and dorm, fine, and I *still* have partial scholarship, but a scholarship for international students was defunded last year—Thanks for your legacy, Trump! My tuition balance has been piling up. I could seriously get deported before I finish my degree. It happens.

"Eight hundred dollars—that's eighty thousand Nepali fucking rupees," I say. If I turn to my parents for help, they'll need to ask for another loan from a relative and lose face in the bargain.

Ali puts his headphones back on.

"What the fuck, I'm talking to you," I say.

"Stop cursing man, it gets old," he says.

"Frequently saying fuck means that you've been here for a while. Start with shit and build your way up. Jerk, dickhead, asshole. When you can say douchebag confidently, you've made it."

"How much do I owe you for these lectures?"

"The whole world thinks refugees are oppressed. But look at you. Milking American generosity."

"Fuck you, man, really."

"That's more like it," I say.

His nostrils flare up in annoyance or anger—I can't tell.

I give him a hug. "My loaded bro," I say.

He shrugs me off and turns on the Premier League highlights on his iPhone 15. The screen on my phone is so damaged, it's practically a flip phone.

When Rashford scores against Chelsea, Ali punches his fist in the air. I punch his shoulder.

He removes the headphones. "Don't ever hit me," he says, the corners of his eyes straining.

"I'm just playing with you, bruh. It's okay," I say, landing another sharp hook on his shoulder. He raises his arm to duck, or to return the blow midair, a second too late. He looks at me wide eyed.

I pull down the visor of my cap and pretend to sleep. I don't feel guilty for bugging Ali, then I feel bad for not feeling guilty, and the permanent halo of calmness that reigns over his head doesn't help.

"I wasn't trying to be an asshole," I say as we walk to the restaurant.

The kid is an old soul trapped in a teenager's body, but I've noticed a change. He walks with the upright posture of an American, not with the usual downcast eyes, as if he were hurting under the load of his thoughts.

I take the football out of my backpack. We pass and kick the ball around until we reach the desolate strip mall rented out to massage parlors and Vietnamese nail salons. From age or negligence, there are cracks in the asphalt, and the parking lines are in need of fresh paint. A Mexican immigrant had recently been caught hiding in an empty dumpster at this strip. The local news had a field day, playing the image of him in a loop as he crawled out of that dumpster. The newscaster had called this the rough part of town.

On the restaurant's rooftop stands a cutout board of a turbaned, mustachioed mascot holding a sign that proclaims Spicy Kitchen in bright red neon. On weekends, I pull double shifts, but business couldn't be worse. Spicy Kitchen has three Yelp reviews with one star each. Some-one wrote that our restrooms don't have hand soap. Not true. A comment like that can be a death knell for an Indian restaurant in a small town. Then Madam wrote five glowing reviews using fake accounts, but you can tell it's the same person because the spelling errors are consistent.

When we enter, Madam is on the phone with her cousin in California, whom she complains to at least a few times a day. For five dollars an hour in cash and free food, I can't complain. Never mind that Ali makes seven fifty an hour.

This one time two police officers came for lunch. I sneaked past them and hid in the bathroom stall. Some days I think what's the worst that could happen if ICE comes after me: an international student, legally in the country with no criminal record, trying to make an extra buck? Then I think, I'm Brown, I have a beard and an accent, and I *am* break-ing the law, or at least bending it. If I'm packed away without a degree, I'll be that person in Nepal who couldn't "make it" abroad, constantly peppered with sympathy smiles.

"They're not ordering from DoorDash also," Madam is saying on the phone.

"Good luck," Ali says, heading into the kitchen.

"Did you brainstorm any marketing ideas?" Madam later asks me.

"Put momos on the menu."

"This is an Indian restaurant. Not northeastern."

"Oh, like this is Indian but not Assamese or Manipuri. By the way, momos are from Nepal, not the Northeast."

"What are some trendy food apps?" she says. "Aren't you the computer science major around here?"

I'm pulling the dusty bag out of the vacuum cleaner. "We need to optimize our SEO, manipulate the algorithm. As soon as someone types India we should be the first name that pops up on Google."

"And why haven't you done that yet? Since you so confidently think of this place as yours too."

I go outside and slam the bag at the dumpster to blow away the dust. Even when its empty, the dumpster smells of dead rats. When I go back in, I say, "At least someone here makes an attempt to go to college."

"I run my own business without student loans," she says. She's from Delhi and she constantly reminds me that most servants in Delhi are from Nepal. "You're the Mexicans of India, na?" she likes to say, but I'm in possession of the one thing she secretly wishes she had—an American college education, and I flaunt it. It's a strange way to bond, putting each other down like that.

"I'm reading *Orientalism* by Edward Said. You should read it," I tell her. "It's about European colonialism dating back to the Renaissance. A lot of tips about how to oppress the poor."

"Interesting. Is the carpet clean yet?" she says. She's counting cash in the register, wetting her thumb once on the yellow sponge. She rearranges rolls of coins, as if that softens the blow of bad business.

Her husband comes out of the kitchen and walks toward the window. We call him Chef. He has a brooding nature, and he constantly complains about something or the other, going outside every hour for a smoke break.

"Coming to this country was a mistake," he says. "Look at the murder rates. No wonder we don't get customers."

Madam throws a quick glance at me. She says her husband's gloom is un-American. She says, "You can learn something from anything." On slow days, which is every day, Madam sits at a table by herself and reads self-help books. When she's lost in concentration, she plays with her earlobe. She once caught me looking at her. She held her gaze for a moment before her eyes fell back on the book. Then she looked at me again and I looked away.

I often hear her arguing with Chef behind a closed door, followed by a long silence that lingers, creating a pool of distress in the whole place. On days like that I wish she'd draw me into her confidence, share her fears, her secrets.

"Why do you think they don't have kids?" I ask Ali in the bathroom. I'm wiping down the sink and he's scrubbing the toilet. The owners don't like to see us doing nothing, so we spend a lot of time in the bathroom shooting the breeze.

"Maybe they don't have a sex life," he says. We laugh.

Sometimes Madam comes on weekend mornings straight from Costco, wearing tight yoga pants. I help her unload stuff from her truck—frozen vegetables, meat, eggs. She's brisk, always on the phone, making "business calls," but I think she really just talks to her cousins. And then I'll find her sitting by herself, playing with her earlobe, staring at the carpet for a long time.

"Why do *I* always clean the toilet?" Ali says.

"Because you make almost three dollars more than me."

"You all are racist against Africans."

"Stop saying that."

"It took you forever to remember I'm from Somalia, not Kenya or Ethiopia!"

"Worry not, brother. In the eyes of America, we're worse than the third world. You know what's funny? Millions of Nepalis would give their right arm to move to Mexico. If Mexico wasn't next to the American border, it would be an immigration dreamland."

Ali shakes his head. His ironed shirt is draped over a hanger hooked on a peg on the bathroom wall, and his white undershirt is spotless and wrinkle-free. I wonder if his formal attire is his way of reminding others that he is not the refugee they might imagine him to be.

"What about you? You can't work here forever," I say.

"I start high school next year." He sprays Clorox on the mirror above the sink. "My father owned a servicing garage in Mogadishu. We are Majeerteen, from a good family."

"Spray. Scrub. Flush. You sure are taking your family legacy forward."

"At least you folks are good company. Did I tell you I applied for a job at Whole Foods in Park City, but they said I didn't have the right experience? I think they were scared that I would steal their organic vegan gluten-free spinach quinoa." He kisses his fingers like an Italian chef and we both laugh.

"Why is your father not with you?" I ask.

Ali dunks a mop into a bucket, then lifts the mop, letting the solution drip on the floor. As he starts mopping, the smell of formaldehyde fills up the room. He's quiet long enough for me to realize this was not a good question.

"I'll handle this," I say, taking the mop from him.

As I'm mopping, I'm thinking, we don't choose life. Life chooses us. "I'll protect you, man," I end up saying. "My bro from another ho."

"That was a joke," I say and slap his head in a friendly way.

He takes a swing at me. I jerk my head back, saved by a split second.

Chef barges in and tells us to get back to work. Ali removes his shirt from the hook and leaves.

Chef watches me as I wring out the water from the mop with my hands and toss the dirty water from the bucket into the toilet. Although I'm shaking, I don't show it.

"Why do you waste so much time with the African?" Chef says.

I ask him to step to the side, using a wet paper towel to wipe his footprint from the mopped floor.

"I can fire you and keep him," he says without any expression on his face.

"You can't because your wife makes all the decisions," I say.

The air is sucked out of his face. "Fucking Nepali," he whispers in foul-smelling breath.

While I stand outside the stall, he takes a shit. The crude sounds reverberate in the walls, and the smell rises, stealthily at first, encircling me like a ring. When he finally comes out, the smell has seeped into my skin and will never wash off. "Hi, I forgot to flush," he says.

The giant piece of shit, curled up like an animal, sits comfortably in the center, feeling superior to me. I need to flush it twice. I stand in the stall, trying to tame the anger overwhelming me. I'm not angry that he humiliates me but at the recklessness with which he does it. If I tell my friends in Nepal that I work for Indians, they'll get offended. This is why. Indians treat Nepalis like shit in India, my friends say. They call us slanty-eyed chinkis. Our entire existence reduced to a humiliating word—bahadur, security guard. A nice word that otherwise means brave, turned into a slur. Poor Nepali migrants—brave and muscular, but brainless. But I try to reason with my friends that not every Indian is cruel, and then Chef tries his darndest to prove me wrong. Every day. But you know who I feel the most anger toward? My own country for not having the power to protect me, for being so utterly poor.

Later, after I've cooled off somewhat, I send Ali a text. *Sorry, bro,* I write, wishing I could send a thumbs-up emoji on my decrepit phone. Surly for our own reasons, the four of us are in different corners. I'm trying to read du Sautoy's *The Creativity Code* for class. When I go out for a breath of air, I find Madam talking on her phone.

She's wearing a black shirt with the top two buttons left open, the splits on her breasts faintly visible. Her hair is tied back to reveal jhumkas, her long Indian earrings.

After she hangs up, I ask her, "Do you think Nepalis are brave and muscular, but brainless?"

"Of course not. What's up with you?" she says with a faint smile.

"Never mind," I say.

After a pause, she asks, "Saturday night and you're reading a book?"

"I have a boring job if you didn't notice," I say. What I really want to ask is how she ended up with a grouch like Chef. Any bitterness I might have against Indians fades, if not entirely disappears, when I'm with her.

"So, when will you introduce me to your girlfriend?" she asks. "Or will that be a boyfriend?"

"Girlfriend, thanks. I'm working on it."

"No Nepali beauties in your college?" Her attentiveness is on full display.

"There was one girl. The only other Nepali. She transferred to U of Oregon."

"After you showed up?"

"Very funny. I stayed because I was promised a full ride. I'm saving every penny I make. Hopefully next summer I can work here full-time?"

"We need to do something about this restaurant, Bikram. I'm counting on you. I wish you were just a little more proactive, you know?"

"I work really hard. More than Ali, to be honest."

She gazes pensively at the mountains. "You know what scares me? We're in debt, Bikram," she says. "The cracks have been showing for a while. I do a good job of covering them up like scars, but you know what happens to an untended scar, right?"

"You're an extraordinary person. I know you'll turn it around."

"Really?" She looks at me almost slyly, as if reading my eyes for a note of deception. "That's sweet of you," she says.

There's silence and I think she senses me looking at her.

"Go help Chef."

"To do what?"

Her eyes harden instantly.

"Got it," I say and head back in. Chef is nibbling on a stale samosa. "What's the cricket score?" I say, trying to coax him out of his sullenness.

"Don't even bother."

Around seven, as if miraculously, an old White couple walks in. The man is so old I can see the veins on his scalp, but he has a set of full white teeth like Joe Biden.

Chef and Ali go into the kitchen as Madam turns on the TV that's screwed on to the wall. A Bollywood song bursts out like a harsh glare, and Madam fumbles with the remote control to lower the volume. I sit the guests down. The woman has frizzy white hair and bright eyes. They're inquisitive about the menu and ask questions about different dishes.

"In ancient India, the local sages would spread tiny bits of turmeric on their bedsheets to ward off evil spirits," I say. "To this day turmeric is a cure for arthritis. Here we use it in most of our curries, but I would recommend the House Special Chicken Tikka Masala." Never mind that this creamy, orange monstrosity is not even Indian. It's Chef's ready-made gravy.

"Sounds wonderful," they say.

"How spicy?"

"All the way to Bombay," the man says with a laugh.

They order two glasses of Argentinian malbec. In the kitchen, Chef turns on the oven ventilation and clanks the big frying pan with a spatula, asking Ali for the spices.

I light a candle for the guests and make a show of pouring the wine into their glasses, unscrewing the cork, making the wine flow carefully, the label facing the guests. I've read that even with a fifteen-dollar bottle of wine, indulging them in the ritual usually guarantees at least one more order of the drink.

They eat slowly, enjoying the water running down their eyes and noses. The occasional laughter rises over the soft raga that Madam has decided is apt for the moment. Ali hovers around avoiding eye contact with me. I tell him, "Look, I'll apologize to you a thousand times. But you look like you're staring at them. Why don't you fill their water glasses?"

He goes to their table with a jug.

Madam comes out to say thank you to the old folks. "What a lovely evening. We don't think we've cried so much," they say, waving as they leave. The overall mood has turned light. Chef keeps saying that he should have added a splash of lime in the chicken. It feels like we just entertained some guests in our private house.

Soon enough, though, the couple is back.

"Did you see a small black purse with a Saint Laurent monogram? I swear I brought it with me," the woman says.

We bend over and look under the table, remove the chairs. The woman stands with a tense expression.

"My purse hasn't left this room. I have a sixth sense about these things." She throws a glance at Ali, making it clear where her suspicion lies.

When he looks at me, Ali's eyes are pleading, but my heart is throbbing with a weird mixture of support and doubt.

"I'll talk to him," I say. I grab his arm, pull him to the side. His face muscles tense as he frees his arm from my grip.

The woman calls 911. "I'm reporting a case of theft," she says.

After she hangs up, Madam says, "There was no need for that. Have you looked in your car?"

All of us just stand there. The man rubs his wife's back. She asks for a glass of water. Madam signals at me with her eyes. When I give the woman a glass of ice water, I notice the blue veins in her neck, carrying the weight of her head, buckling under the thoughts that live there. I'm so nervous I'm paying rigorous attention to detail, as if my brain is telling me to concentrate.

"Evening, fellas." A White police officer shows up. He is charming in a well-oiled way, the kind of charm that makes people uneasy. His partner, his backup, sits in the car, its blue-and-red lights flash outside the window. A Glock, pepper spray, and taser are hooked on the officer's belt. He writes down our names on a yellow pad and asks the couple to look for the purse in their car. While they're gone, the officer angles his face to talk into the mic clipped on his shirt, as if every chatter and dispatch being transmitted all over the country is describing us. I feel trapped in a room that suddenly feels airless.

"Under the car seat," the man says, waving the purse as he walks in.

"Ugh, I'm so sorry," his wife says.

"Please don't come back," Madam tells them.

The woman looks offended. An embarrassed smile creeps up her face. She pulls out two twenty-dollar bills from her purse and leaves them on the table. "I meant no disrespect. I'm so sorry." She lowers her voice when she says this. They get out quickly.

The cop asks us for identification. Madam says, "You should go after them for humiliating us."

"Just a routine check."

My heart is pounding. When the illegal Mexican was caught in the dumpster, he was pie-eyed, hiding from cops who found a half-pint in his dashboard during a routine stop. He had been in the country for two decades, with a law-abiding family. It was all over because of one mistake.

The backup officer walks in. Ali promptly pulls out his state ID and green card from his wallet. The green card surprises me—people don't usually carry it with them. The officer collects their cards to run them by the computer in the car.

"What do you do?" the first officer asks me. When I tell him I'm not carrying an ID, he asks for my social security number.

"Isn't that outside your jurisdiction?" Madam asks.

"You could be in trouble for hiring illegals," he says.

"He doesn't work here. He's my cousin."

"Does he work here?" the cop asks Ali.

"No," he says, looking terrified.

"I go to SUU, officer. I don't remember my social security number," I say. "It's in my dorm room."

The other officer returns. "All good," he says, returning the documents.

The first officer gives Madam a business card. Maybe it's a reminder that he'll be on our trail. "Sorry for the trouble, folks. Have a good rest of the day," he says before leaving.

I don't know if it's the relief of not being handcuffed, but I feel a step removed from reality. I go to the bathroom and sit on the toilet, holding my legs from shaking.

"This motherfucker," Chef says when I come back out. It takes me a second to realize that he's talking about me, not the cop. "Like a politician who doesn't bother to stab you from the back. They smile at you while they're killing you," Chef says in Hindi, fully knowing I understand every word.

"Bas," his wife says.

"Not the simple Nepali. This one is dangerous."

Madam grabs the forty dollars and gives me twenty.

"I worked more than eight hours today," I say.

She hesitates, folds the other bill with a sharp crease and passes it to Chef.

"Don't come back here for a long time," she says.

"Am I being fired?"

"There's something wrong with you," she says. "Throwing that boy under the bus like that. There was no need for the police to be here."

For a moment I had wondered if Ali had indeed taken the purse. I didn't entertain the thought, even briefly, that the woman may have misplaced it. They had seemed too nice to be sloppy or prejudiced. Now, I'm thinking, where would Ali have hidden the purse even if he had stolen it? I guess my mind was racing in so many directions, I couldn't see what was in front of me.

"Can we talk at least?"

"No. That gora has his eye on you," Madam says.

She doesn't show any sign of paying me the balance. "Can I get the other twenty?" I ask.

"Give it to him," she tells her husband, as if doing me a favor.

"Thank you for everything," I say, surprising them both. Instead of bitterly arguing, I end up blurting out a noble response to mask my despair.

Madam's eyes reveal a nervous tenderness, and I'm overcome with a feeling that I've never been able to read her motivation.

Ali and I walk to the bus stop, on a dark, narrow street with cracked sidewalks. The open field stretches out for miles. There's a barn and a smattering of houses. Occasionally I hear wind chimes.

Ali walks with his headphones on, carrying a plastic bag in which carefully wrapped pieces of naan are stacked with a chicken dish that he is taking home for his mother and sister. He removes the headset to talk loudly on the phone in Somalian. He sounds anxious, but it could also be a normal way of talking. Will he ever forgive me? I don't know.

The first thing I'll need to do is check out all the books assigned for next semester from the college library. Then plead with the financial aid office, who'll send me the standard email with links to private loans—"You might want to speak with so and so." Anytime they say, "You might want to" without giving a direct answer, you know you're screwed.

When I'm hit by pangs of anxiety, I have strange dreams. Mostly, I dream of an outbreak of dysentery. It's always the same story. Someone sells bad milk in the neighborhood and all the children die, their tummies bursting like balloons. My eyes will suddenly open, relieved that it was only a dream. I'll look at my phone, 3 a.m. I'll go on Craigslist. 7–11? Gas station? They don't take a chance without documents anymore. I'll fall into another scattered dream. It's usually my parents waiting for me at the airport, the acrid sweat of humiliation dampening their armpits.

After he finally hangs up when we reach the bus stop, Ali looks at me and says, "I pity you." I could have reacted any which way: arguing, fist-fighting, apologizing. We just missed a bus and the next one is an hour away.

"Let's go to McDonald's. My treat," I say.

He follows obediently. Inside the brightly lit joint, I order two Big Macs, fries, and Coke. I ask him what else he wants. We eat silently, wolfing down our burgers.

"I feel sorry for you," he says.

"You already told me that. Don't you have anything original?"

"Asshole."

"Good. One step closer to citizenship," I say.

He takes out the naan and chicken and we dig in, dirtying our hands together, eating from the same plate, sharing the chicken and fries.

"Eat, eat," he says, putting some of his fries on my plate.

After a while, I muster the courage to say, "I shouldn't have done what I did with you. I'm sorry for that."

He scans my eyes. "Which part?" he asks.

"I wasn't trying to insinuate anything."

"I don't have my dictionary, Bikram."

"Indirectly blame you. That wasn't my intention. It was a natural reflex."

"In the morning, you accuse me of being loaded. Come evening, I'm a thief."

He lets that sink in.

"What will you do now?" he says.

"Kill myself."

"I'll do you a favor," he says. "I don't want to work in that place any-more. I'll stay until the end of this month. She'll call you back. They're too cheap to hire anyone else."

Is he being generous, condescending, or both, I wonder.

"You don't have to," I say, not meaning it. I know that if he quits, that would be a lifesaver.

There's a new hardness around his eyes, tempered by the wisps of hair that will not grow into a mustache on that childlike face. "I'm not *just* doing it for you. I want to start a new life," he says.

"Congratulations."

"Not even a thanks?"

"Gracias, señor!"

He rolls his eyes and I flash a smile.

Next to our table is a McDonald's refugee sleeping in a sitting posi-tion, surrounded by her bundles. Ali wipes his fingers and takes out his wallet with multiple pockets. He puts a twenty-dollar bill on the woman's table.

"You asked me about my dad," he says. "You want to hear the story?"

"Now?"

"It helps me remember."

"Sure."

"We owned a servicing garage in Mogadishu. But my Aabe also taught sign language to deaf children in his spare time. He always thought about the poor. We were rich, let me tell you. We had a house, a car. I went to a nice school. When Al-Shabaab came to our town, they demanded money from contractors and business owners. Aabe didn't give in, so they killed him as a friendly warning to others. We fled to Kenya—me, my mother and sister, in a private taxi in the middle of the night."

He takes a sip of Coke.

"Lying on my cot every night, I would hear children playing outside our tent. I became mad at my Aabe for abandoning us. As the eldest son, I have duties, Bikram. I need to protect my family. I haven't come this far to let people like you humiliate me."

The silence weighs me down. He takes time finishing his Coke, slurping all the way to the bottom.

"The way you treat me is awful. But I know you're not such a bad person," he says.

When he goes to the bathroom, I slip out and pick up the twenty he left for the woman. But I feel horrible about it and put it back on the table on my way out.

We wait for the bus in silence, trapped in our own secrets. One of my favorite novels is *Purple Hibiscus* by Adichie. It's a commentary on how White colonialism disrupts a Nigerian community. I got an A+ in that class. As the only Brown person in the room, I became a trusted voice against racism—even the professor's ears perked up when I talked, but I'd never actually met an African before Ali. If I wasted food as a child, my mother always pulled a guilt trip by saying, "Some kid in Africa is starving." Never mind that millions of Nepali children starve every day.

Am I jealous of Ali? Yes. Would I tease him if he were White? Probably not, but I also wouldn't feel any connection.

"At least I have one bragging right," I say. Rashford scored first, sure, but it was Chelsea who won the game. Palmer with the winner. A touch, a fake, a cut, and a smash into the net.

"Let's stay in touch. At least to watch the game together," I say. I almost punch his arm but end up patting his back.

I don't know what triggers him. But he punches me in the face, so hard that I'm blinded for a few seconds. When I open my eyes, I see him walking away.

Kali

One day, my father returned home from work with a puppy. It was curled up in the nylon bag that normally carried his office files.

"Found it behind the Nardevi temple. Not more than a month old," he said. The puppy looked like a fruit that had fallen off a tree.

"Have you gone crazy?" Ama said, perturbed by the timing.

"It'll be good for us," Father said.

Father, or Buwa as I called him, worked as a registrar for a wholesale distributor of shoelaces. The walls in our rented flat had never known the smell of fresh paint, and the 21-inch TV was switched off most of the time with an eye on the electricity bill. Only the sofa spoke of an elegant intention, with its hand-carved wooden frames and Dhaka-patterned cushions. The sound of traffic ceased when you sunk into it.

Ama's concerns were valid. Our alley had been on overdrive to shoo away every stray that found its way in sniffing for an opportunity for food or shelter. The government's scheme to "Take the Bite Out of Rabies" came with a cash reward of ten thousand rupees for the cleanest alley in each municipality. The question of how the cash would be distributed among neighbors hadn't been considered nor had anyone given a thought to the government's ineptitude to fairly dole out such a reward. For our lower-income alley, however, the announcement seemed ripe, bursting with promise, and our neighbors, though hardened cynics, couldn't ignore the temptation.

47

We found out later that a sterilization scheme proved to be a cover-up to kill entire canine populations. Kathmandu's stray dog problem would be tackled with brooms and sticks, and eventually mass poisoning.

~

After dinner, Buwa lay on the sofa, resting his feet on Ama's lap. Ama was knitting a sweater as she did every night. Some nights, she massaged Buwa's toes, clipped his nails. I was on the floor doing homework under a 40-watt bulb hanging from a wire, though my eyes kept straying to the cardboard box in the corner where the puppy slept.

"Think of him as a new family member," Buwa said.

"As if we don't have enough worries without the neighbors getting on our case," Ama said.

She had gone through a difficult pregnancy with me, which the doctor thought was the main reason for her infertility. They had wanted a second child not only because of the anticipation a new child brought, but a single child betrayed societal expectations. After the diagnosis, Ama and Buwa went to shamans, knocked on temple doors, consulted priests. Buwa eventually sought refuge in his transistor radio and Ama poured her frustration into the cauliflowers and cabbages that she shredded with her rusty knife. I was a ten-year-old surrounded by silence and homework.

"By the grace of God, we're blessed with a son. We don't need another child," Buwa said.

Ama pushed his feet away.

"Son. Daughter. It's the same thing," he said and put his feet back on her lap.

That night, I pressed my ear against my bedroom door and slowly opened a crack. The puppy wailed and Ama held him after some hesitation. It cuddled snugly into her arms. Next morning, Ama boiled milk in a steel tumbler and put it next to the cardboard box padded with a blanket; the puppy finished off the milk until the tumbler rattled. Ama named him after the four-armed goddess—wearer of human skulls, destroyer of evil.

"But Ama, he's a male," I said. I wanted to name him Spidey or Batman, a name I could boast to the neighborhood kids.

"Kali it is," she said.

Of course, the neighbors weren't happy. First, they complained about the wailing, then the incessant barking, but our ultimate fall from grace happened when Kali pooped in the alley, and in front of everyone, Ama casually picked it up with a plastic bag and walked twenty meters to a roadside dumpster. "Infertility is not a disease, but it kills you mentally," they said as they watched Ama hold the defiled plastic that she was prudent to tie with a knot.

Time seemed to fly, and Kali grew into a huge mongrel, a cross between a mock German shepherd and a hodgepodge of breeds I couldn't identify. He had a shiny black coat with soft brown patches. In our tiny living room, he jumped from chair to chair, chewed on rubber slippers, and chased his own tail. We fed him mutton gizzards and bones. To cut costs, Buwa also made a rule of no sweets for the rest of us when we took Kali to a veterinarian. That embargo sometimes lasted for a month. If Kali rolled in the dust making a thorough mess of himself, Ama and I bathed him with scented Lux soap under a tap and checked the roots of his fur for lice. Ama also knitted a red bow with pretty folds and tied it to his collar.

Our flat sat above a sweet shop. By daybreak, the alley would get crowded with noisy officegoers and our flat heavy with the smell of milk tea and fried samosas. Because Ama never complained, Ramcha, the sweet maker, returned the favor with the occasional free plate. Something deeper than tenement papers, an unspoken trust, bound them, but the arrival of Kali changed the dynamic.

Ramcha had been the most vocal anti-stray proponent in our alley. Anytime a stray found its way in, he would fling a broom, forcing the dog to scamper off with a growl.

"Kerosene. That's the trick to chase dogs away," Ramcha would tell me when I was on my way to school, about a twenty-minute walk from our flat. Although our science teacher lectured us about animal rights, in our alley, where the houses were pressed together, any talk of animal rights stank like a taunt from a roadside garbage. Ramcha was muscular, and he liked to force himself into kids' soccer games. He also saw himself as a community organizer, often holding meetings in his flat to discuss ways to improve the alley. These meetings became more frequent since the government's announcement of a cash reward. Strategies were discussed and discarded with extra urgency. Some suggested sprinkling vinegar instead of the more expensive kerosene. Others proposed taking turns to guard the alley with sticks— the government inspector made random checks and a show of intent would send a strong message. "Why don't we pool money and build a gate?" others suggested, an idea that was shut down by Ramcha, because ours was a commercial alley. In his sweet shop, Ramcha also sold daily necessities like cigarettes, candles, biscuits, and in the corner of the shop, he cooked fresh samosas and tea for officegoers who came from neighboring settlements. His vendetta against strays was especially piquant because he was concerned that an unclean shop would drive his customers away, and he took Kali's arrival as a personal snub.

A few houses away from ours lived an eighty-year-old widow. Everyone called her Tol Ko Muwa, or Alley's Granny. She wore a faded cotton sari and a pair of old rubber shoes. She had a slight limp and after every few steps she stopped to gather her breath, often resting her arm against the wall for support.

Every day Tol Ko Muwa went from house to house, talking about a time when her life was filled with riches and joy. Out of sympathy, people's doors remained open for her, which gave her easy access into their lives, and she scattered their secrets sparingly, like throwing a handful of seeds to a flock of pigeons. She also had an uncanny ability for timing her visits—arriving at one house during lunch, landing at the other at teatime.

It was around three that Tol Ko Muwa usually came to our house, by which time I would have returned from school. Even as Ama went about doing her chores, Tol Ko Muwa would sit cross-legged in a corner and chat away. While recounting her glorious past, her tone was nostalgic, and she placed her hand on her head, but when she gossiped about the neighbors, she was secretive, whispery, leaning closer and waving her wrist to emphasize a point. Sometimes Ama left the room and returned after ten or fifteen minutes, but Tol Ko Muwa continued complaining and mumbling like nothing had interrupted her, until Ama put a plate of roasted peas and a cup of tea in front of her.

"Was a time after marriage when we ate mutton every day," Tol Ko Muwa would say, or she'd talk about the days when her feet touched nothing but high-heeled sandals that her husband bought from the fancy shops of New Road. "And these days? People can't even afford rubber slippers. That Durga bahini's slipper snapped and she hooks it with a hairpin."

Tol Ko Muwa had organized a prayer ceremony in her flat for interested neighbors to sing and pray for mother's fertility. The plan didn't materialize because Ama refused to partake in it, though that didn't stop the older woman from prophesying another son in Ama's womb.

"Why does she care when her own children never visit her?" I asked Ama.

"Such thoughts are not worth dwelling upon," she said.

Tol Ko Muwa tried talking Ama into getting rid of Kali. "Accepting one's fate is knowing one's place in the grand scheme of things," she said, adding that a black animal, especially, could be inauspicious. When Kali ran to her wagging his tail, she reached for a broom.

"He is just trying to know you," Ama said, snatching the broom from her. As Kali grew bigger, he had to be put on a leash when Tol Ko Muwa visited. Chained to the landing of the staircase, his bark echoed in the neighborhood.

Our alley teemed with children with whom I played soccer after school in a nearby field. By the time Kali was a few months old, however, there was only one thing I was impatient about—when would Buwa return so we could take Kali for a walk? To bide time, I helped Ama clean the dishes. She washed, I wiped. She had hung a string of plastic bulbs over a small portion of the wall facing the sink. She liked to hum old filmy tunes as the blue-red lights danced like glitter. I would join her occasionally, throwing the melody off-kilter, though that never stopped her from saying I made her proud despite my awful voice.

As soon as we took Kali out, the neighbors froze on the spot, narrowing their entire concentration on the dog, but their children, my friends, wanted to leap forward and hug Kali. Everyone stopped what they were doing and watched, because Kali looked like an Alsatian, known to be bred by the police purely to scare the poor away. Or so we thought because of the images on TV where the police would attack the homeless with snarling Alsatians on their leashes.

Away from the alley, though, on a leafy road lined up with nice houses, people stopped to ruffle Kali's hair and inquire about his breed. Evening joggers or toothless porters, no one was denied a wagging tail. Street dogs sniffed the air and attempted to follow us for a few paces, eliciting an irked growl from Kali. We felt like royalty, as if we were riding on a chariot, offering a smile here and a nod there.

Meanwhile, there was a garden that Ama had told me about. She had been there once, before I was born. It was a beautiful place, she said, full of flowers, where the wind blew from faraway fields. The image of this garden lingered in my mind, but it was some ways off, and Buwa was worried that if we went too far, stray dogs might pick up a scent and follow Kali back to our alley. He didn't want to upset our neighbors more than we already had. Still, during those walks, Ama and Buwa tried to match their steps with Kali, and their skin no longer looked tired. Buwa even convinced Ama to go to a hairdresser. They argued about the cost, but after much cajoling, Ama went in. While we waited outside, an open van full of caged strays sped down the street and parked across from us. Two men emerged and threw a blanket over a dog sleeping on the pavement. When she was released into the cage, a cacophony of barks erupted, playing havoc with Kali's temper so he whined nonstop. Ama came out smelling of jasmine, her hair elegantly coiffed. "My queen," Baba said, glowing with pleasure.

~

One day after school, I decided to take Kali for a walk by myself. Perhaps my teacher's "very good" at the bottom of a report card had stirred my confidence. I hooked the leather strap to his collar and off we went, running down the stairs, even as Ama was calling me from the kitchen. I made sure to hold firmly to the strap and kept telling myself to be alert, but as we passed by the sweet shop, the fragrance of the freshly cooked lalmohans captivated me. I stopped to savor the aroma of those perfectly round sweets that Ramcha arranged like a pyramid on the glass shelf. Kali was pulling on the leash, perhaps restless to get to the main road, but the rich smell of lalmohan had found me, and now it lingered under my nose. Ramcha told me to shoo the dog away, but I was unable to take my eyes off the liquid syrup dribbling down my favorite food. "Just for you," Ramcha finally offered me a free lalmohan. As I hurried to claim my prize, Kali's leash snapped.

The lalmohan splattered on the ground, its syrup trickling into a crack while Kali ran around the alley, whipping out his tongue. People scampered and hid behind whatever they could find—garbage cans, electric poles. Some even went inside shops.

"Don't run," I said when Tol Ko Muwa came from around a corner, carrying a bowl of rice pudding. Kali went after her. She tripped on a stone and the bowl shattered. Kali snarled at her, mist spraying out of his nose. He then appeared to dig his teeth into her thigh but quickly backed off. After I grabbed his collar, people surrounded Tol Ko Muwa, shouting at the top of their voices. When she pulled her sari up to her calf, there it was: a redness around teeth marks but no sign of blood. "Rabies!" someone screamed, though I tried to convince them that Kali had no such disease because he had been tested.

Ramcha carried Tol Ko Muwa in his arms, and with the help of two other men, he rushed to the main street and hailed a cab.

Later that evening, the neighbors gathered in our flat. They all sat on the floor except Ramcha, who sat on an upturned bucket. Tol Ko Muwa lay on the sofa, a bandage wrapped around her swollen calf. The neighbors chipped in for her treatment, the largest portion to be covered by Buwa. Kali had grazed his teeth without actually biting the old woman. While we waited for Buwa, Ama knitted silently. Every now and then she went to the staircase, where Kali was chained to a railing, and measured the pink crocheted pattern on Kali's back. People poked their heads out of the door when she did that.

"We have seen how the dog has ruled over your lives," the sweet maker said as soon as Buwa entered.

Buwa looked at Ama to indicate he would like tea. Ama went to the kitchen and Buwa took her chair. He fanned himself with his crumpled topi. For a while no one spoke, and the sharp flame of the kerosene stove could be heard from the kitchen. Ama reappeared with a tray filled with glasses of tea for everyone.

"Listen, bhai," Ramcha said to father. "We've been living together for over ten years. This alley is our home. When you're in need of money, I have helped you, have I not?" He paused, letting the effect of the sentence settle around the room. Fresh murmurs arose. People looked at each other, then at Buwa. "Now, you're letting Kali run wild, putting our lives at risk."

"He's just a dog, not a tiger," Buwa said.

"What if he shits when the inspector visits?" someone asked.

"We always clean up after him. And, by the way, when has the inspector ever visited? This whole scheme smells like a scam."

"The issue is," someone said, "Kali isn't just a dog. He is an Alsatian."

"He's a mongrel," Ramcha said. "A gutter dog can't be scraped into an Alsatian. That's my issue."

He then spoke slowly, looking straight at Ama, as if their trust was being tested. What about all the hard work to keep strays off, he said, and if by accident, Kali attacked one of his customers? Courage was about making small sacrifices in the present for a more promising future, he said, surprising us with his eloquence.

This went on for a while. The few who said keeping a pet shouldn't become a cause for argument were shut down by Ramcha. In his youth, Ramcha had been a wheeler-dealer who made money on the side by helping people get what the government made difficult: driver's licenses, citizenship cards, permits, and now he made a case that with a few right moves, the reward was ours, and with it, perhaps a new streetlamp in the alley so someone like Tol Ko Muwa wouldn't trip in the dark. It was hard to argue against that. The last one to leave, Tol Ko Muwa clasped her hand in Ama's, relishing the opportunity to remind us that we were lucky to live in such a close-knit neighborhood.

In the evening, due to a power outage, we sat by a candle.

"You should have been more careful. You're almost a man now," Buwa said.

"Don't blame him," Ama said.

"We must pretend that he ran away somewhere," Buwa said, trying to convince himself. "Dogs are dogs after all. We searched behind every temple, every shop, but he outsmarted us—simply went seeking a better life."

Kali lay on the floor with his tail down, ears perked back. After a warm dinner of bone broth and rice, he came to my room as he did every night. I wanted to cuddle him, but a part of me was relieved at the thought of letting him go. I couldn't match the happiness he brought to my parents. I wonder if he knew that because there were nights when we stayed in my room without speaking. I would not respond when he licked my hand or brushed his wet nose on my cheek. Now, he slept on the edge of my bed, one eye cocked toward me.

My parents argued late into the night. Why hadn't Buwa told Ama about borrowing money from Ramcha? Did *she* know anything about Kali's expenses? The dog didn't go anywhere near vegetables, and gizzards didn't grow on trees. The last veterinary bill after Buwa fed him chocolate and he vomited all night—that bill turned the leak in Buwa's wallet into an aggravating drip. He was still counting the splashes in his head, he said. Didn't Ama understand anything just because he shielded her from the truth? She accused him of being selfish not only about Kali, but about everything else that had ever hurt her. Why did he sit on her chair when she went to make tea earlier in the day? Where was he supposed to sit? he said. Did he notice that she had to sit on the floor? Long after the embers in their voices had dimmed, I lay silently in bed, petting Kali, and just when I thought he was drifting off to sleep, he got down on the floor, leaned on his elbows, and arched his back, challenging me to a game.

"I'm tired," I said, and he climbed on the bed next to me.

I woke up to soft, distant knocks.

"Time to go," Ama said.

As soon I opened the door, Kali wrapped his legs around Ama's. She was wearing Buwa's old tennis shoes, a mismatch with her sari.

"Please, Ama. He's our Kali," I said.

Her flesh had tightened underneath her skin. She tied Kali to a leash while Buwa wiped his glasses with his shirt.

"Perhaps leave him at the temple. Someone will pick him up," Buwa said. But Ama was already out the door.

The alley was buzzing with the morning din. A vegetable vendor who plied his trade on his bicycle sprinkled water on spinach to make it shiny. Ramcha shouted at him to take his wares elsewhere. "This is a clean alley," he said. "We don't want your litter."

When he saw us, Ramcha asked us if we were indeed doing what he thought we were doing.

Ama didn't respond. She held my hand, and Kali sniffed the ground as if the inevitability of his fate was taking shape in his mind.

I was filled with hope when we walked past the temple. I was now a few steps behind them. We kept walking. Until we reached the garden.

We had to pay a fee at the gate. First, I saw a lily pond. Then shaded walkways covered with vines, fountains with lion heads next to which foreigners practiced yoga. A parallel row of angled bricks curved like a snake across the grassy terrain, creating a long, narrow path where chrysanthemums blossomed in purple. Soft music played from speakers hiding in bushes. Under the blue sky, Ama let go of the leash. Her steps were measured and awkward, relocating to a ground long forgotten. When she gathered pace, the hem of her sari, secured to her blouse with a pin, fluttered in the wind. She ran with her eyes closed; chin pointed to the sky. Kali barked happily and caught up with her, as if he wanted the same thing she was after. I too sprang into motion, and we ran without a direction, toward and away from our hopes and fears.

Ramcha's expression soured when he saw us. Ama had the firmest expression I have seen on her face, holding tightly onto Kali's leash, warding off any look meant to stir a residue of guilt. But it was Buwa's response I was concerned about. I knew he secretly pined for Kali's return, though he seemed surprised. "But . . . ," he said when Ama stopped him.

"For once, we're doing what I decide," Ama said, and from that day onward, she put her foot down to get what she wanted.

Buwa sighed. As soon as Kali ran to him, however, the anxiety dissipated from his face, and I came to accept that our lives would be filled with immeasurable joy and controversies with Kali in it.

In the months and years ahead, pakoras continued to sizzle and tea continued to simmer in Ramcha's shop. Tol Ko Muwa initially avoided eye contact, and some neighbors spat out globs of phlegm when we passed. Eventually, life resumed as it had been. The government's scheme turned out to be a fake promise with no evidence of cash prizes ever being handed out, and Ramcha had to work harder to keep up with the competition from a big franchise sweet shop that had opened up branches all over the city, including in the leafy road close to our alley. Their lalmohans were stuffed with pistachios and topped with silver dust, and every month, Buwa saved up enough so we could enjoy a small family outing, treating ourselves to some luxurious sweets. We would follow that up with Ramcha's freshly brewed, thick milk tea. He couldn't afford to fill his lalmohans with pistachios, or infuse his tea with ground cinnamon and cardamom, so he relied on time-honored, simpler ingredients like sugar and a few seeds of black pepper that he would toss into the simmering pot of tea. We also drank his tea, of course, because we didn't want to cut off all ties with him. Though

Ramcha had stopped sending free plates of samosas to our flat, he would attempt to engage Ama in small talk, but she kept him at a polite distance.

Occasionally, when we passed by him on our evening walks, Ramcha would mock Kali for being a senior citizen in dog years. Sitting cross-legged behind a huge iron cauldron in which he deep-fried his sweet, crispy jeris, Ramcha would yell, "There goes the pampered prince." Kali would turn up his nose, defying the sweet maker's petty ire. He knew, after all, that it was his barks that kept thieves and hawkers away from our alley.

A Short Visit

Nirmal hugged his father at the airport. It had been three years since they had seen each other.

"I had an enjoyable flight. Long but enjoyable," Baba said. He looked thin and unrecognizable. His speech was slightly slurred. Nirmal didn't want to read too much into that, because he didn't want to entertain the possibility that Baba might have had a few drinks on the plane. After the intervention, Nirmal had thought Baba's drinking had long been a thing of the past.

On the drive to a restaurant—Nirmal hadn't had time to cook—Baba said that he'd had a beer and a whiskey on the plane. After a long silence, Nirmal said, "Why?"

"It helped me sleep," Baba said. "But I'm on vacation, so a few beers is okay. I drink at weddings in Nepal. You can ask your mom."

Nirmal was sure that was a lie. Ama would have told him on the phone if he'd started drinking again.

At the restaurant, Baba said, "Why don't we get a beer?"

Nirmal got annoyed. "That's not going to happen after all that you've been through," he said.

Baba became morose and ate quietly. Despite some anxieties about spending three months alone with his father, Nirmal had looked forward to Baba's visit. They bonded over politics, books, Nepali cricket, and at this moment, there was so much else Nirmal had wanted to ask his father. What did he think about the six-lane highway? The decor in this fancy Nepali restaurant with the water-spouting lion by a koi pond? Nirmal's shiny black Tesla? All those things that someone visiting America after ten years would normally comment on. Nirmal had played in his mind the Denver hotspots he would point to on their drive from the airport. His father would quietly admire the grandiose complexities of America, ask numerous questions about gun violence, BLM protests, all those images on TV, but Baba didn't seem that bothered. He sat in the car lost in his own thought. A quiet fear tickled Nirmal. He knew that his father had only one thing on his mind.

The sulkiness continued for the rest of the day, and Nirmal tried to blame it on the jet lag. When he went down to the kitchen the next morning, Baba had fixed himself a cup of tea and sat on the dining table reading an old copy of *Kantipur* he had brought from Nepal. He didn't show any desire to move from that chair. Nirmal had taken two weeks off from work, the second week won after a hard bargain.

"Breakfast?" he said. He made an omelet with onions and cilantro, just the way Baba liked it, and served it with black coffee and toast. Baba made a comment about getting a mild shock when he touched a light switch. "Is the house properly grounded?" he asked. It was, as far as Nirmal knew. He had never given it a thought, though.

Later they went to the Museum of Nature and Science and walked quietly, each observing the exhibits on their own, making perfunctory comments along the way. It had only been a day, but it already started to feel like Baba had been here longer. The plan was for them to spend the summer together. Nirmal now wondered if his father could cope without Ama, who wasn't able to come due to visa issues, and he worried that they would get on each other's nerves even in his 2,500-square-foot house. He was working from home these days, which, he now thought, may not have been the best of ideas.

When they returned home in the evening, Nirmal said, "Okay, just this one time. I'll get a six-pack for old time's sake. But it's just this one time."

"Fine with me," his father said, no doubt beaming internally, though he didn't show it. Nirmal knew he had opened the floodgates. He hoped he wouldn't have to regret it too much. He bought a pack of Blue Moon because it wasn't as strong as an IPA or dark as a stout. A lemon rind would add the light touch. At home, he chopped carrots and cucumbers into little pieces with chicken sekuwa from the night before on the side.

They raised their glasses and clinked, making brief eye contact. This was how they bonded in Nepal when Nirmal made his regular home visits, about once a year, before the divorce. His older sister, Binita, was always busy with work and with her family, and most of his school friends and cousins had left Nepal for greener pastures, so his dad had become a reliable companion during those short trips.

A soft glow emanated from the beer glasses. A few sips later, Baba said the sekuwa tasted very good. He talked about Nepali politics. There had been a mayoral election and Baba was optimistic about the new leaders, a crop of young enthusiasts. Nirmal tossed chopped onions and edamame on the pan for a stir-fry. He asked his father about Prachanda, Oli, and the whole corrupt bunch of leaders. By the time they finished the six-pack, Nirmal thought, *That wasn't too bad.* He had looked forward to this conversation. No one had insights into Nepali politics like his father, and few could shoot the breeze as well as he. If they paced themselves, the odd drink here and there might grease the wheels during the initial days.

The next day, they didn't think twice about picking up a bottle of gin, a case of beer, as they drove to Wash Park. Though alcohol wasn't permitted in the park, people drank out of red cups. It wasn't that uncommon. Nirmal spread a blanket next to a picnic table and a barbecue pit. It was a beautiful summer afternoon. They laid out a spread of crunchy spicy snacks they had picked up from the Indian store, as well as a box of Vietnamese summer rolls, tortilla chips, and guacamole. The drinks were in a cooler.

"I only drink a few beers or glasses of wine on weekends in my normal life," Nirmal said. It felt important to make that clear. They sipped their gin slowly and chased it down with beer. This time, it was Baba who asked a lot of questions, about Trump and the general state of American politics. Nirmal enjoyed explaining things about America to his father. Baba laughed heartily at the embarrassment that was Trump, though Nirmal pointed out that democracy was increasingly at stake in America.

Occasionally, they fell into a long, comfortable silence, admiring the view of the boathouse and the distant lure of downtown Denver. At some point, the conversation shifted to Nirmal's work, the dog-eat-dog culture of the tech industry, his quick rise as a software developer at CyberGRX. Nirmal knew his father was proud of his son's career, but Baba wasn't generous. It was important for Nirmal to share details about his struggles and success with his father, face-to-face. This was another conversation he had played numerous times in his mind. Nirmal hadn't had the chance to *show* Baba just how well he was doing. The alcohol loosened him up. He recounted an argument with a colleague who had suggested that a native speaker should present a demo to the client, insinuating something about Nirmal's accent. The argument had turned nasty when the colleague said Nirmal was overreacting. Despite a large number of South Asians at the company he worked for, Nirmal frequently felt lonely and anxious. He was aware that his struggle seemed trifle to his father, who belonged to a generation that had lived, and continued to live, a life in Nepal where water shortages and acute pollution were common. People struggled to make ends meet, and poverty and politics were things to reckon with. But he wanted his Baba to recognize his struggle too. He wanted Baba to acknowledge that his life in America was no less daunting, and his success was a thing to be proud of. "I'm proud of you, son," he wanted his father to say, but Baba didn't say that. Instead, he asked, "Why did you get a divorce?"

Nirmal was thrown off. He was prepared for this question, just not so abruptly. He had planned on opening up. Give Baba a few days to settle. There wasn't much to say, and their story was one of many. He and Katie just sort of drifted apart. They had met in grad school and decided to marry soon after graduation. When Nirmal landed this job in Denver, they made the move from the East Coast. After a year, Katie was hired by a public policy firm in DC. It was her dream job. They gave long distance a shot, but it didn't work out. It happens. People grow and change. They didn't have kids and there were no strings attached. They were still friends, and that was the important thing. Nirmal's parents had warned him about marrying a White woman. But it wasn't like that. It wasn't anyone's fault. She wasn't better or worse than a Nepali just because she was White. Not Katie.

Baba poured himself another drink. He was a greedy drinker, the type who recaps the bottle and pours a little bit more before closing the cap again.

"Santosh is another sad story," he said, referencing a cousin who had also gone through a divorce in Australia. "I hear he's addicted to anti-depression pills."

"What do you mean *another* sad story? You think my life is sad?" Nirmal asked.

"Of course you are pidit," Baba said, using the Nepali word that hit close to the bone. There wasn't an English word to convey the level of sadness contained in that word. Pidit was a gnarly entanglement of aggrieved, depressed, victimized.

"That's so not fair," Nirmal said. "I was hoping that you would look at the bright side. See how much I've prospered despite the divorce."

"You are a lonely man," Baba said. "I know it, and I knew it as soon as I entered your house. It smells barren. It smells like a house where a woman or a child has never set foot. We were so worried that you are living in depression. Are you?" His shoulders hunched, and he started to cry.

Nirmal didn't know what to do. Theirs wasn't a hugging relationship. He couldn't even remember when he had last seen his father cry, and now he just watched Baba cover his face in his palm, sobbing like a child. He moved closer, put his arm around his father. "Don't cry, Baba, please don't cry. Please, I beg you," he said. He became conscious of how drunk he sounded. When the crying stopped, Nirmal removed his arm, because he wasn't sure what the appropriate gesture was. Rubbing his father's back felt too intimate. A pat too formal. Baba wiped his eyes with a tissue.

"It's just that you married in haste. We only met Katherine once in Nepal. We never got a chance to know her, or love her, accept her as our own. And the next thing we know is you both want a divorce. We were told on the phone like it was the weather report. We felt so left out in the entire course of events. We are simple people, unequipped to deal with this American way of life."

Nirmal had not bargained for a guilt trip. His parents had always made things about them. The standard tropes about them being deprived of grandchildren, a dutiful daughter-in-law, had been repeated time and again. In Nepal, divorce was a defeat. It was more their defeat than his.

"Look, I'm only thirty-nine. I'll find someone. People in this country get married in their fifties. Or some people never get married and are perfectly happy. Each to their own." Nirmal moved back to his spot and opened two cans of beer. He passed one to his father.

"Is that what you want? To never marry again? You sound like an old gypsy trapped in a forty-year-old body. You've always been a philosopher. Zero practicality."

"Thirty-nine."

"You'll be forty next month," Baba said. He took a long sip of the beer. Silence descended between them like a fog. Nirmal ate his summer rolls quietly, dipping them in guac.

"Come on, let's go for a walk," he said later. They had polished off half the gin. "A bit of exercise will do us good. We can leave the stuff here." He closed the chip packets with clips, shut the lids. When he stood, Nirmal realized how properly buzzed he was, and it wasn't even one o'clock yet. He extended his hand and helped Baba to his feet. Baba stumbled for a second and almost fell before finding his balance. In the restroom, they peed side by side, staring at the white tiles, listening to the sound of their piss hitting the water in the urinals. Walking back, Nirmal knew exactly what they needed. He asked his father to wait and darted off to his car to pick it up. Sledding was a fantastic idea. Of course it was!

They walked up a slope. Nirmal took out a can of beer from his pocket, cracked it open, took a swig, and passed it to Baba. Hiding it in red cups had ceased to be a concern. They passed the can back and forth. When they reached the top, Nirmal sat first and held the grip.

"What are you making me do? I'm too old for all this," Baba said.

"Believe me, you won't regret it. Sit behind me and hold on to my waist."

Baba did as he was told.

"Not like that. Stretch out your legs. Hold steady . . . shoot, wait," Nirmal said and tossed the empty beer can next to a tree. He then pushed the sled forward a few steps with his legs. When they were on the edge, he said, "Ready?" and down they went, dropping like a roller coaster, screaming all the way. They toppled over when they reached the bottom. Nirmal found the whole thing so exhilarating, he couldn't stop laughing. Baba lay flat on his back, but he was laughing too.

"Want to do it again?" Nirmal asked, mildly dizzy.

"You're crazy," Baba said.

They lay on the grass, staring at the sky.

"So, Katherine didn't mention anything about my email?" Baba asked.

"Which one?"

"After the divorce. I sent her a long email. I blamed her. I told her she had ruined my son's life. Bitch."

"Whoa, whoa," Nirmal said. "One at a time. First of all, don't ever call my ex-wife that. Are you *drunk*?"

Baba became quiet.

Secondly, Nirmal thought, he was hearing about the email for the first time. He was terrified of what else Baba might say.

"She shouldn't have married you if divorce was always a viable option for her."

"It wasn't her decision alone. We both decided it," Nirmal said.

"It's a cultural thing," Baba said. "Would you have been so casual about it if you had married a Nepali woman? If divorce is a possibility, people will latch on to it at the slightest inconvenience. Marriage is not a game of who blinks first. Not for us."

Nirmal almost leapt with anger. Of all the difficult conversations he had anticipated, this had not even entered the realm of possibility.

"How could you do this behind my back?" he said. Katie hadn't mentioned anything. It wouldn't have mattered one way or the other, so she probably shrugged it off, but this was embarrassing and not fair to her.

"Did she respond?" he asked.

"She unfriended me and your mother on Facebook. That was her response."

The combination of alcohol and this revelation made Nirmal's head spin. He ran to a bush nearby. The bile from his stomach traveled backward through his digestive tracts, tormenting his muscles, and splattered on the ground. He sat on his knees for a while, expelling deep, dry breaths.

His father stood behind, gazing down, as if he were hoping that Nirmal would look up and make eye contact. Nirmal brushed past him.

"That was intrusive, Baba. You had no fucking right to do that," he said in English. He had never used the word before in front of his father.

"We have every right to be worried about you," Baba said after they sat down again.

He poured a shot of gin and passed it to Nirmal. "It'll tame your stomach," he said.

Afterward, Baba slept on the blanket in a fetal position, his small frame appearing frail. They drove back to the house in the evening well after Nirmal felt relatively sober. His father's words still burned around the edges of his temper. He turned up the music in his car to break the silence.

Next morning, Baba said, "It was a bit much yesterday. All that drinking. Sorry if I said anything to hurt your feelings."

"You should apologize to Katie," Nirmal said. "You really shouldn't have called her that."

"I didn't call her that in the email. I apologize to you, son, and if you say so, I will apologize to her. It was the alcohol that made me say that word. You still have feelings for her?"

"It's not about that. My feelings don't matter. You really should say sorry to her for the email," Nirmal said again, although that was easier said than done. He rarely talked to Katie anymore. They texted each other occasionally and liked each other's posts on Instagram. She was in a serious relationship, which made Nirmal mildly jealous because Katie still looked beautiful in those pictures with her dimpled smiles, but Nirmal had, for the most part, moved on. It would be beyond awkward for his father to call her now and apologize. He decided he would reach out to her one of these days.

When he was making breakfast, Baba walked into the living room—which was adjacent to the kitchen—with a basket full of laundry and started folding their clothes, including Nirmal's underwear.

"What are you doing?" Nirmal said and snatched the pair of boxers from his father. It was one thing for his mother to do things like that—she still treated him like a child—but it was extremely awkward to see his father fold his underwear with tiny avocado prints.

"Let me help you while I'm here," Baba said.

"You can help me cook, but really don't worry about any of that. You're here to relax. I'm used to cooking, cleaning. A maid comes every two weeks for deep cleaning, anyway. It's no big deal."

"Is she Asian?"

"She's an older woman from Guatemala. Don't even think about it."

"I'm only saying because if you give her a little extra money, she will cook for you. These maids do that."

"It doesn't work like that in America," Nirmal said.

Later that morning, they got on a Zoom call with Ama and Binita. Binita's children and husband showed up to say hi before going to sleep. Ama was staying at Binita's house for the duration of Baba's visit. When they asked what father and son were up to, the men said they went for a drive up the canyons. It was actually Nirmal who made it up. Baba played along, giving him a conspiratorial look from the corner of his eyes. Binita later sent Nirmal a text on WhatsApp: *Keep him away from you-know-what.*

The intervention had happened about a year ago, when Baba got drunk at a wedding party in Kathmandu and slumped on the floor, his zipper open, the tip of his penis exposed. For most of his life, he was what could be described as a chronic drinker, possibly a functioning alcoholic—Nirmal couldn't discern the difference. Baba drank five whiskeys before dinner every night, quietly, watching the news on TV, but wasn't beyond bingeing at parties, and had become somewhat notorious for tripping and falling at inappropriate moments, forcing Ama and Binita to stay vigilant at all times. At this party, Baba apparently walked out of the bathroom and passed out, most likely having forgotten to zip up his pants. Binita and her husband had to lift Baba up, put him in their car, and drive away, leaving behind a trail of gossip. The next day, they had the intervention, chiding Baba that enough was enough. His drinking was no longer just a health hazard, but an embarrassment to the family, especially Binita's kids, who stared quietly at their grandfather when he made a scene. Nirmal, who was busy at a weekend conference in Aspen, couldn't FaceTime them, but Binita had implied that Nirmal was negligent, and also, perhaps, lucky that he had never had to deal with their father's escapades. Nirmal was the one that went away to America while they were left to deal with capricious behavior, alcohol-induced whining, and daily embarrassment. Baba was usually a quiet, nonviolent drinker, but he had this annoying habit of muttering to himself when he was inebriated, lately about Nirmal's divorce, and Nirmal, feeling complicit somehow, had done his part by sending money, as he did every month, but he sent extra money in case Baba needed medication or therapy. When Ama's visa fell through and Binita was reluctant to send Baba on his own, it was Baba who insisted that the trip was the change he needed. Nirmal seconded the decision, because why not? It was an opportunity to hang out, just father and son, get to know each other better.

After the Zoom call, Nirmal avoided any topic about alcohol.

"Let me be the in-house chef today," Baba declared and walked to the store, bought bags of groceries, and prepared a sumptuous meal—Nirmal's favorite, no less: black lentils, alu kauli, and saag. He completed all the chores, even scrubbed grease off the gas burners with soap water. In all fairness, Baba shared cooking and cleaning responsibilities with Ama even back home in Kathmandu. Nirmal's mood lightened at the sight of Baba's cheerfulness, and he thought it best to put the Katie incident behind for now.

After lunch, they lazed under the patio umbrella, drinking iced tea. "Cost me four thousand dollars." Nirmal pointed to his high-end Lynx grill. Baba poked and prodded and decided that the flame was low. For a man who had never used a barbecue grill, it was a stunning display of confidence, the way Baba dismantled the parts and changed the frayed wiring. He also complained about a leaky faucet in one of the four bathrooms that no one used and offered to look at it while he was here.

Nirmal sensed a veiled judgment accumulating through the myriad observations.

"Let it be," he said. "I'll call a handyman."

A displeased shadow cast over Baba's eyes. "I'm tired. I need a nap," he said and went to his room, leaving Nirmal to wonder if his father was jealous of his success. Baba had lived frugally on a bureaucratic Nepali salary, his electrical engineering degree laid to waste in offices crammed with dust-covered files.

Nirmal and his sister shared a room until they were teenagers, listening to each other's breathing. When Nirmal left to pursue an American education, he had been freed from a space of shrinking possibilities, unlike Binita, who stayed back because someone needed to look after their parents. Binita had taken the high road apparently, a responsibility that naturally fell on a girl's shoulder as she liked to hint, but it wasn't Nirmal who had asked her to put her dreams on hold for their parents. She could have left if she wanted to, as many siblings did, and their parents would most likely support her. They would eventually figure out a way to accommodate Ama and Baba in their lives. Binita had done very well for herself in Nepal, though, with a master's degree in architectural engineering, a high-paying consultant job, and marriage to a man she loved with children she adored. But an air of tension always hovered between them, because one of them had made the bigger sacrifice.

As the day wore on, Nirmal's craving for a drink steadily increased. He was on holiday too. Shouldn't that count as a credible reason for a beer, maybe two? Truth was, he couldn't go to sleep without a few drinks with dinner after an exhausting day. He was so immersed in his work that it took the familiar amber of a single malt to send the slow tentacles of awareness through his body, awareness about the rest of the world that included sports, politics, and silly videos of bungee-jumping accidents on YouTube. He had cleared out his bar for the visit, but now, he retrieved a bottle of Glenlivet XXV from his bedside drawer and poured himself a drink.

By the time Baba came down to the living room, Nirmal was properly flushed in Scotch and beer. He'd taken the bottle downstairs. Baba appeared disappointed at first, then that unmistakable glint. He poured himself a Scotch and they spent the rest of the evening watching the Nepali version of *American Idol*, nursing their drinks, snacking on leftovers from lunch and Thai takeout.

Their lives fell into this rhythm. Nirmal and his father spent their days either lazing around the house or visiting the city's landmarks, buoyed by the drinks consumed intermittently throughout the day. Evenings allowed for more drinks with dinner. Nirmal steered the conversation to neutral topics like politics and sports—he even took Baba to a varsity baseball game. Katie, who had grown up in a baseball-crazy family, had inspired in him a love of minor league and varsity games. Nirmal hadn't been to a game since the divorce and he took extra pleasure in explaining the rules to Baba, who listened with keen interest, wanting to be mesmerized by this American phenomenon that his son so enjoyed. Baba kept up the pretense by cheering with a raised beer glass every time he heard the crack of a bat. When Nirmal's neighborhood school, Denver West High, won a game, he hugged his father in a spontaneous outburst. It was on the drive back home, when the excitement of the game still lingered between them, that Baba abruptly told Nirmal about a divorcee in Nepal who might be a potential match.

"At least listen to what I'm about to say. What is it with this wall of silence? Is everything okay with you? With your body?" Baba asked.

Nirmal said, "I don't want to repeat the mistake by marrying in haste."

"But who will marry you if you keep waiting for a full moon? Should you also be driving after drinking so much?"

"I pace myself well. I'm a responsible drinker," Nirmal said, and added that he frequently took an Uber if he crossed his limit. This was not entirely true, though.

One evening, Nirmal discovered that the medicine in his bathroom cabinet had been moved around, including the orange bottle of Prozac. Even more embarrassing was finding out that his father had seen Katie's picture, stuck to the edge of the mirror, but flipped over, so that Nirmal only saw her face if he opened the cabinet. On the side of the photo that faced Nirmal when he looked at the mirror were the words, *Today will be a better day.*

Nirmal felt it was time to have a conversation with Baba. He was incensed, but as he crept closer to his father's room, he heard him talking on the phone with his mother.

"He has no friends," Baba was saying. "I haven't met a single person since I've arrived. And what is the point of making all this money when I see him wearing the same pair of jeans every day? Isn't that a sign of depression?"

Nirmal's shoulders sagged. He walked back to his room. He realized that no matter how much he tried to laugh, his father returned to a sadness like a ghost haunting an old shirt. It sounded harsh to admit, but the only word he could think of was disappointment. He was disappointed in his father and couldn't help but wonder if the trip had been a bad idea. Nirmal didn't need reminding that he eventually needed to find a partner, that he didn't have a great social life, that he was working himself to the ground, that the drinking could be handled better, that he, as his therapist said, suffered from a milder form of dysthymia, yet none of those things, individually, had tilted over the edge. It wasn't even dangling on the precipice. He wasn't so depressed that he struggled to leave his bed in the morning, and his drinking certainly didn't affect his work. He had pulled it together for the most part, and he derived a lot of happiness from work, and wasn't that the whole point of life, to find your own happiness?

"Please stop intruding in my life," he said to Baba over dinner. "The email to Katie, the nosing around my medicine cabinet. When will it stop?"

Baba was not affected though. "It will stop when I'm convinced that you are on the right track," he said.

"At this rate you will never be convinced until I turn into a version of yourself—a resentful, petty man who begrudges his son's freedom."

Baba's eyes narrowed. He took a long breath. "You are already turning into a version of me, and that is what I don't want to see," he said.

Nirmal knew exactly what his father meant, and he didn't have the perfect retort. His heart pounded, he was desperate for a drink, but he resisted, not wanting to show any sign of weakness. "I'm more successful than you could ever imagine, and you can't handle that," he finally said. Baba said nothing. It turned into a tense, silent dinner.

Nirmal went for a drive, without a destination, fighting the urge to go to a bar. He regretted snapping at his father. When the regret coiled into a knot and lodged itself in his chest, it made Nirmal agitated. He hit the steering wheel with his palm, then took three long breaths, allowing his breath to leave his body gently each time. He parked outside a Walmart. The good news was, his vacation was coming to an end in four days, and even better news popped up on his phone. Nirmal, who went to Nepali parties only occasionally, was delighted that he and his father were invited to the wedding anniversary of one of Denver's well-heeled couples—an opportunity to leave the house.

Baba was reading under a lamp in the living room when Nirmal returned well after midnight.

"You should stop driving after drinking," Baba said.

"Why are you still awake? And I didn't drink. I was eating this in a parking lot outside Walmart. You want some?" Nirmal said, shaking a tub of ice cream.

"Katherine had warned me, you know. She called once and said you were drinking too much. I told her she worried too much, without realizing the extent."

"Good night," Nirmal said.

"Eat less ice cream," Baba said sarcastically. "It pumps up your blood pressure."

"We're going to a party on Saturday," Nirmal replied in a singsong voice.

∽

At the party, Sabina made eye contact and held it, a trait she no doubt picked up from her job as a marketing exec at Cigna in New Jersey. She was visiting a cousin in Denver.

"Also divorced," Baba said when he introduced Nirmal to her.

Nirmal winced.

"I heard you're a software developer?" she said.

"Yes," he said. Nirmal had gone out of his way to say hello to everyone, laugh at all the jokes. Though he wasn't a fixture in the Nepali community, he enjoyed the occasional gathering, and he wanted to show Baba that he was no recluse. Father and son made a pact to keep an eye on each other and stay out of drinks to prevent word from reaching home; for Baba's sake, Nirmal said he would cohere, though the bar that had been set up in the foyer was proving too enticing to ignore.

Nirmal wasn't sure how Baba found Sabina. He must have surreptitiously looked at women he thought were single. As Nirmal and Sabina fell into easy conversation, Baba made a strategic exit.

"Sorry if my father pried into your life," Nirmal said.

"Not a problem at all. My parents are the same . . . constantly worried," Sabina said with a smile.

He told her about his job and noticed that she moved her thumb up and down the stem of her wineglass when he talked, focusing her concentration on his every word. She too talked about her career, living in Jersey, the daily commute to New York City. She said she wanted to move out of the jam-packed East Coast.

"So how long have you been divorced?" she asked.

"Two years. You?"

"A little over one."

The half smiles felt like a recognition of a shared experience.

"Attention, folks." The emcee then made an announcement. Anyone new to Denver had to go on stage and introduce themselves. Sabina graciously volunteered to go first. The crowd cheered her on. She kept it short and sweet. As she walked back to where Nirmal stood, he was struck by her beauty—the soft big eyes were a sensual mismatch with the perfectly toned body. Nirmal made a signal with his thumb that he needed to use the restroom. This was a good time to make a pit stop at the bar because most of the guests were streaming back into the hall for the anniversary couple's felicitations. Nirmal ordered two Maker's Mark double shots and bottomed up. Just as he was about to make his way back, he saw his father in a hallway near the back exit, taking a swig out of a tall glass. Baba looked like someone's driver at a wedding

in Nepal, cowering in a corner, scrounging on leftovers. Nirmal wanted
to confront his father, but it would be too embarrassing to walk in on
each other.

When Baba staggered on to the stage, Nirmal was certain that there
had been a few more drinks. Baba took the mic.

"Are new people still introducing themselves?" he asked the emcee.

"Sure. Why not?"

"Brothers and sisters," Baba said. "My name is Narayan Kumar
Dhungel. I'm a native of Dillibazar, Kathmandu. I'm so happy I made
this trip to visit my son." He pointed to Nirmal. Some people in the
crowd acknowledged Nirmal with a nod or a thumbs-up. Baba became
silent. The microphone discharged a squealing static sound, and Baba
stood still for almost three minutes. The crowd started to murmur, and
the couple who were celebrating their anniversary stood on the edge
of the stage and looked surreptitiously at their watches. Nirmal was
about to go to the stage when the emcee said, "Sir, if you're finished,
can I have the mike?"

"Hold on," Baba said, pointing his finger. "I will always love my son.
Thank you." He walked off the stage to a smattering applause.

Sabina, standing next to Nirmal, kept her graceful posture, without
a hint of reaction, which made Nirmal more self-conscious. He smiled
at her.

"I really wish you had controlled yourself. It's only a matter of a few
hours," Nirmal said, pulling Baba to the side.

"Just one drink. No one noticed."

They watched the speech quietly. "I'm sure it was more than one,"
Nirmal muttered. Baba was trying to keep his palm from shaking. He
got those alcohol shivers when he gulped down quick drinks.

Sabina, no doubt hearing the exchange, excused herself to go to the
restroom. Nirmal went to the bar.

He asked for a shot and gulped it down. His father followed.

"What are you doing?" Nirmal asked.

Baba looked at Nirmal like he was judging him.

"Let's just go," Nirmal said. He kept shaking his head in the car,
hit the steering wheel with the heel of his palm more than once. He

would've liked to say goodbye to Sabina. It was rude. She had noticed the awkwardness.

Nirmal went up to his room the minute they reached home.

"What about dinner?" Baba called out. They hadn't eaten much besides appetizers.

"I'm not hungry. You can eat whatever is in the fridge," Nirmal said.

He made himself another drink and lay in bed, scrolling through social media to find Sabina. And there they were. Pictures of the party already posted on Facebook. Baba huddled in a corner with a glass of beer. In fact, there were a few of Baba, mostly out of focus, covertly standing in the background. But, in all of them, he had a different glass of alcohol in hand, seemingly unaware of being caught in the frame. Who had posted it? Nirmal couldn't place the name, but she was friends with Binita. He made a few calls to get the pictures of his father removed, but to no avail.

In less than twenty-four hours, Binita arranged for Baba's return ticket. She called Nirmal twice that night. The first call was brusque. Had he seen the pictures? What was going on? Where was Nirmal when Baba was drunk? Baba wasn't drunk, he tried to reason.

A few hours later, Binita called again, as if there was no more fight in her. She said she had been skeptical of sending Baba, knowing that Nirmal was no teetotaler. She had seen him drink on his vacations in Nepal but chalked it up to just that—holiday drinking. She thought she had enough faith in her brother that he would put aside his recreational needs for his father's sake, for his family's sake, but he had proven just how irresponsible he could be. She said she was deeply disappointed in herself for trusting him. They were so proud of Baba for finally quitting. She had even convinced him to go to therapy. Had he said anything about that? No, he hadn't. Of course not, she said. She gave no indication that they had any inkling about Nirmal's own drinking issues.

In the morning, hungover and cradling a mug of coffee, Nirmal remembered saying sorry to Binita. It sounded hollow. Ama would eventually come around, but he felt like something had changed in his relationship with his sister. Add to the mix the fact that his brother-in-law wouldn't be okay with what had transpired.

Father and son sat at the dining table, Nirmal with his coffee, Baba with a bowl of oatmeal. Both lacked the conviction to tell Binita that Baba should stay longer.

Baba spoke first. "You know why I was so persistent about drinking the minute I set foot?" he asked.

"Go on."

"Because I thought that was the only way we could be comfortable with each other. Since you have become an adult, we have rarely had any meaningful conversation when drinks weren't involved. Your mother and I sometimes feel that we invade your privacy if we ask too many questions. But I wanted you to tell me about your issues. I'm your father."

"What issues?"

"I had a feeling you had a problem. But you are discreet like me, a solitary drinker. No one can really find out because you've built a wall around yourself. I thought you would finally talk to me."

Nirmal realized that his father was shifting the blame. His anger turned in a slow current in his brain.

"Baba, you've been acting like a parched dog, constantly sticking out your tongue, since you landed. I tried to control you," he said.

"You're not going to hurt me, son," Baba said after a pause. "You know what's funny? In Nepal everyone thinks how successful you must be with your big house and fancy car. Your mother knows you might have a problem, but she's in denial."

"I don't need this right now," Nirmal said and walked away. He shut his bedroom door and rummaged through his medicine cabinet. He took a Valium to calm himself down, then he lay in bed almost breathless with anxiety. He felt a quick, sharp pain in his chest. After some hesitation, he called Katie.

"Is everything okay?" she asked.

"I wanted to apologize for that email that my dad sent you. I just found out. He's here for a few days."

She was silent for a while, then she said, "I would have liked to talk to him, but it was so . . . vitriolic."

"I'm so sorry. I think he was confused and angry."

"Blame it on the woman, right?" she chuckled sarcastically. "You know what? Never mind. How are you doing? How's your health? How's the . . . drinking?"

"I've cut down a lot, actually. Only drinking on weekends."

"I'm glad to hear that," she said. "I hope you're getting the help you need, Nirmal. I really do. And while your dad is there, tell him the real reason. Tell him that your drinking was what really ate into our marriage. Did you tell him that?"

He felt that shitty unfriendliness their conversations could unexpectedly spiral into.

"I just called to apologize. I know Baba was out of line. Won't happen again," he said.

She sighed then said, "I appreciate that. I'm glad you're doing better. I hope only good things for you, Nirmal. You're a good man. Don't be too stubborn to ask for help," she said.

Just as she was about to hang up, Nirmal said, "Wait. Do you have a minute? My father wants to say hi."

"Really?"

"I think he wants to apologize."

"That's not necessary . . . and I'm not ready for it. Bye, Nir, take care," she said and hung up.

Nirmal was too tired to feel indignation, let alone anything stronger. As the Valium took effect, the storm cloud in his mind unleashed its rain, and a warm glow inhabited his body. He kept looking at the number, as though he wished she would call again, and then the regret of snapping at his father took hold. He knew the regret would multiply as soon as Baba headed toward the departure line.

He slept for a long time, a deep, dreamless sleep. When he went down eventually, Baba was waiting with his suitcases by the edge of the staircase. "Thank god, I woke up on time. I can't believe everything is happening so quickly," Nirmal said.

He carried the suitcases to the car. "Are you sure you have your passport? And the ticket in your email?" he asked.

"Don't worry," Baba said.

The silence in the car was like a dull, throbbing pain that Nirmal didn't know how to break out of. He turned on the music on his phone then turned it off. The interstate green boards for the airport started to appear. Nirmal wished they were going on a long drive. It felt like he and Baba had hardly talked about anything meaningful. Every plan that he had mapped out in his mind prior to the visit—the evening walks, the slow unfurling of topics that had never been broached between father and son—had vanished.

"What you said on the stage that day . . . it was touching." Nirmal put his hand on top of his father's and kept it there. Baba flipped his palm over and clasped his fingers with his son's.

"Take a break for a few months and come back to Nepal," Baba said. "We will deal with our problems together."

Nirmal wanted to appear strong. He wiped tears with the back of hand. Baba gave him a side hug. Nirmal tried to laugh when Baba beamed a smile.

They hugged tightly after Baba checked his luggage.

At the time of leaving, Baba looked into Nirmal's eyes and said, "You need help."

Nirmal looked away. His father released himself from the hug, and just like that, his small frame shrank into nothing as he walked away toward the TSA lines.

On the drive back, Nirmal cranked up Bipul Chettri with the windows open. The air in the car breathed a new life even as it mourned the absence of his father. Returning to Nepal for good was a romantic idea he flirted with occasionally, like every Nepali did at one time or another, but he was too baked in his own ways, his work, his solitude. He enjoyed the American freedom to fester in his isolation. He would DM Sabina. Get to know her. Maybe something would work out.

I live with all my frailties. Looking for a place to be . . . Nirmal sang at the top of his voice as the freeway lights illuminated the interstate under a red Colorado sky, and the button strips between lanes glowed like a string of bulbs. Nirmal knew he would have to ask for help someday. Just like he had always known he had needed it.

High Heels

Sarita was up at the crack of dawn to practice her walk in her new high heels. She just hadn't been able to garner the grace that those Bollywood heroines were famous for. She admired the ease with which they moved their legs in rain-soaked dances, perfectly balanced in their high heels. But when *she* tried, Sarita struggled to stand straight, and her feet burned from the lack of padding in these shoes that she bought at Kathmandu Wholesale.

She knew Binod would notice her high heels because he liked to compliment her when no one was looking. The other day, he said the mole above her lip looked like a tiny juicy grape. The same mole her mother said looked like a tumor. That was Sarita's mother being kind. Well, how low had Sarita fallen, or how fitting, that she now thought a tiny juicy grape was a compliment, especially from a bully like Binod.

He showed up in her dream one night, kissing her, moving his hips up and down between her legs. She was jolted awake into a cold and lonely night, so wet that she was scared it would come running down any minute. Sarita prayed for forgiveness, and many nights after that, she was scared of falling into the darkness of sleep, which didn't stop her from thinking about Binod often during the day, the subtle ways in which he showered attention on her, like those extra minutes after work when he hung around to ask if she needed a ride home, building up her hope until one of his cronies would start whistling, and that's what Sarita couldn't quite figure out—if Binod was sly or utterly false.

When the wall clock embossed with a picture of Jesus Christ struck eight and announced, "Glory be to God," Sarita hurried into the kitchen. She loved kneading dough for roti and slapping it on to a hot tawa, where it puffed up and took on a life of its own. She had stopped caring that no one at work, not even Binod, asked her to join them for lunch.

"Glory be to God," Sarita said as she stood before the mirror knotting the drawstring of her suruwal. A touch of red lipstick and a squirt of Lakmé Elegant perfume later, Sarita slipped into her red high heels. She checked her side profile. She had seen her manager attract a natural awe, as if a person's shoes defined her status. As long as her suruwal covered her legs, Sarita passed the modesty test. Priest Matthew always stressed on modesty. He had made an example out of Sarita when her lipstick fell from her purse one day. Priest Matthew picked up the lipstick and took a whiff of it in front of the congregation and said it reeked of sin, before slipping the lipstick in his pocket. Later, Sarita looked for it in every trash can, and when she couldn't find it, she mustered the courage to ask him. "You're bold," he said and gave it back with a smile.

Presently, with her lips red and her shoes shiny, Sarita sat on the edge of a seat in the tempoo, where sweaty bodies chafed against each other. During this long and crowded ride to work, she played her favorite verse in her mind: Mark 11:25, "When you stand praying, if you hold anything against anyone, forgive him, so that your Father in heaven may forgive you your sins." As soon as she reached her desk at Nepal National Bank, the taunts started.

"Here is Miss Mary," Binod said.

"Mary, when will you marry?" someone chimed in.

Sarita's eyes locked with Binod's. It was as if his gaze were a thing, like a ball he volleyed up to her, daring her to pick it up and throw it back. Then his look became tender like he was privately relaying a message that he had no guts to declare publicly.

Sarita took out the wooden cross from her purse and placed it on her desk. The bank was buzzing already, with customers lining up to collect their money. Sarita and the three men were confined to this crammed remittance room with an awkward table arrangement where her back was perpetually exposed to their crude eyes and remarks. So many times, Sarita complained to management, but they kept brushing it off as a temporary arrangement. Unlike the main section of the bank where a glass partition was fitted from one end to another, behind which clerks sat in their cubicles, the remittance room had no ventilation. It smelled of poor people's sweat.

The rumor was that the manager did not like Sarita's constant chatter about God this and Lord that, but she knew that the real reason she was stuck in remittance was the lack of a college degree. She felt a mixture of awe and pity for her manager, a woman with wealth, education, and a taste for pencil skirts—the steady clatter of her high heels on the concrete floor was enough to put everyone's mind to work, but rumor also had it that the manager declined a promotion because she wouldn't dare earn more than her husband unless she wanted to be a home-wrecker. No matter how many fancy degrees they had, Hindu women preferred to toil under gender oppression. Sita, the self-sacrificing wife of Ram, was always a step behind him, but Adam and Eve were companions as God had intended, for they sinned and repented together. Even Priest Matthew, who displayed an open hostility at the slightest hint of lipstick, said gender equality was what set modern Christians apart from simple-minded Hindus, urging Sarita to bring new women—or men—to church, something Sarita hadn't yet been able to do.

She handed out cash to a long line of people who gave her their secret codes, showed her their ID cards, and collected cash that their relatives, working as cheap laborers, wired from Dubai. Sarita was kind toward elderly customers who didn't have proper identification but brought crumpled letters from their sons as affidavit, and she created a separate line for disabled customers, a policy the bank hadn't yet implemented. They looked at her cash counting machine in wonder, for it could count hundreds of bills within seconds. Like the whirring machine, Sarita's own mind was constantly ticking—a wavering, bumpy path, in need of asphalt, which the church no doubt provided. She considered buying a kilo of rasbharis for the evening mass as a gesture of appreciation, though it was not her turn to do so. Priest Matthew had introduced a new rule where every member of the congregation had to bring an offering as a gesture of appreciation once a month—a small something—that would be of value to the church.

It was Priest Matthew who'd baptized her with the name Mary, a week after he had discovered her and saved her from an eternally cursed life as a low-caste Hindu. The priest had shown up outside their mud-covered house on the outskirts of Kathmandu, two blessed years before, wearing a sharp blue shirt, carrying a Bible and some mangoes. He sat on a mound of hay by the cow shed and read several stories from the Bible, including the one about how the Lord healed the blind and lepers with nothing but miracle and mud. While the rest of her family sat on their haunches sucking on the mangoes, Sarita had been mesmerized by the silver-haired priest, his lilting Darjeeling accent, and his smile, which still lingered in her senses. It was as if he had appeared out of the fog, carrying stories so bright they spread a light in her heart. Most of all, the stories spoke to Sarita of a world where she'd be taken in as an equal by the Lord, not dismissed as a Kami. Just the fact that she could read the same Bible that the priest read, in simple English, was a deal-breaker, because it wasn't customary for low-caste Hindus to read the scriptures, an entitlement granted strictly to Brahmins.

Sarita had always wanted to speak good English, to go to college, but her parents saw that as an ill-disguised attempt at snobbery. Getting through high school alone had been a hard-fought battle. Her mother would time those morning chores perfectly until Sarita refused to wash the pots and pans, which caused her mother to rebuke her endlessly from their mud porch every morning while Sarita walked to school.

Priest Matthew hadn't just read the Bible, he had unfastened a bolt and opened a door Sarita didn't know existed, so despite her parents' fear of the foreign religion, despite the seduction of an endless life roaming and roving the hills and paddy fields she grew up around, despite the prospects of marriage and family, Sarita followed the light.

Her father was a blacksmith who made iron statues and sculptures for a contractor. His dream was to open his own shop one day, which Sarita could help look after. She could clean the shop every morning, arrange the sculptures, fend off stray dogs—all the ways she was expected to put her hands in the water cautiously, then her toes, before jumping into a life devoted to cleaning her husband's house, but her father's request for a business loan was turned down by every bank on grounds of insufficient documents, or insufficient caste—one could only guess. Sarita knew her father could never afford all the equipment to forge metal, could never uncover himself from his moroseness, so she told her father that she wanted to discover her own path. He called her arrogant and other names, but she left her home and rode a bus to Kathmandu city and found a single-room apartment near St. Mary's Church. She volunteered at the church and landed a decent-paying bank job, thanks to that high school certificate she fought so hard to earn.

"How about some coffee and cake, Mary? It's a beautiful day," Binod said. Sarita almost jumped, startled, because she still wasn't used to being called Mary outside her church. It was a name meant to be used by people who treated her as their own. Binod had waited for his lackeys to leave for lunch before approaching Sarita with this proposal, which surprised her because it was a step up. He leaned so close that a whiff of his aftershave assaulted her nostrils.

"I'm busy," she said.

"Actually, I have a genuine question. I'd love to hear about the Bible from you."

Binod was handsome, no doubt, with a clean stubble and easy smile. "We've been working together for almost a year, but I hardly know you," he said.

Sarita shuffled papers on her table. The scripture commends the person who obeys God's laws and helps others obey them at every opportunity. Priest Matthew always stressed this point, and though other sisters and brothers brought new members to the church, Sarita, despite her inner voice setting her on a straight path, had never been granted the opportunity. She wondered if this was a test.

"Sarita?" Binod said, interrupting her thoughts.

"I need to use the bathroom," she said, feeling a flush of excitement at the prospect of going out with Binod.

She avoided the remittance bathroom, where grime had collected on the edges of the mirror. Careful to be out of the manager's sight, Sarita slipped into the bathroom in the main section of the bank. She looked in the mirror, wishing for the umpteenth time that she had a lighter skin tone. It was one reason she carried a tube of Fair and Lovely in her purse all the time. She now rubbed it generously and urgently on her face. She hoped he would ignore the mole, sticking out like a nipple, and focus on her pretty smile and the black hair that fell straight and proud below her shoulders.

"Well?" He was waiting.

As they walked the long aisle of the bank, heads turned. Sarita took small, measured steps, trying to strip away a vision from her mind of how jealous her female coworkers must be, in their two-inch heels and flats, too timid to wear high heels for fear of offending the manager, or their mothers-in-law. Sarita then felt guilty for harboring such petty feelings. But her mind was buzzing with so many thoughts, like a stirred-up bee's nest, that she hadn't even noticed that they had already reached the parking lot.

She had seen Binod's swanky motorbike from afar. It was shiny and black with sharp edges all around and the passenger seat was elevated as if it were a mating call.

"What do you think?" Binod asked.

She was mesmerized by the various buttons.

"As long as we get back on time," she said. "I hate to keep my customers waiting."

Minutes later, they were out on Ringroad and Binod sped faster and faster, and Sarita's heart beat like it was caught in a tornado. She screamed but she couldn't hear her own voice, so she ended up laughing at her silliness. She clutched the metal bar behind the seat with both hands as he swerved in and out among trucks and cars and Sarita felt her heart swinging in her chest and a rush of blood explode in her veins. She screamed into the wind in delight and fear, but just as soon, she realized that in a moment of weakness, her hands had left the bar and were tightly wrapped around Binod's waist. She withdrew her hands, and not knowing what else to do with them, started punching his back, begging him to stop, stop, STOP!

Binod stopped outside a dusty restaurant on the highway. The place looked like a crumbling mansion where ghosts of the Rana kings and queens might climb the creaky stairs at night. There was no one for miles except a lone waiter standing by a table with a fly buzzing around him. A quiet fear clutched at Sarita.

Out in the back was a circular veranda overlooking the sprawling Kathmandu valley: old brick houses and ancient temples jostled against high rises of cement and steel, spread out beneath the blue hills. Sarita hadn't realized they had ridden all the way up here.

"I come here alone when I need to get away," Binod said.

Their table was one of many lined along the arch of the veranda. A patch of bougainvillea harnessed to the railing reminded her of dry corns that hung by the windows of her village house.

Binod ordered two coffees and fruitcakes. He took off his dark glasses. The other day, Sarita had made him the subject of confession at church. She had played this scenario endlessly in her mind—should she, should she not, and finally, without naming names, she asked Priest Matthew about desire. She stressed that she simply wanted to understand teachings on self-control. Priest Matthew said sexual union should be saved for marriage, when the couple would enjoy mutual pleasure and be fruitful and multiply. When Jenny asked her who the guy was, it hurt Sarita to know Priest Matthew had shared her confession behind her back. Like that time when Sarita had brought a poster of the Virgin Mary holding baby Jesus in her arms. Priest Matthew had praised Sarita's astute judgment in selecting the finest poster and had even complimented her, in front of everyone, then later when she was alone, almost breathing into her ear. She had felt uncomfortable, but she couldn't turn to anyone, least of all Jenny, who Sarita found out much later was Priest Matthew's favorite. In a crowded room, his eyes always wandered toward Jenny, a pretty girl from a middle-class Christian family in Kathmandu. Apparently, her family had "connections." He had struck Sarita off his list as soon as she landed in the city. When she searched for his eyes,

Priest Matthew looked away. He only looked at her when she wasn't paying attention. He kept his remarks short—"You look better with your hair loose" or "Don't forget to clean the windows." The more glamorous work of maintaining the church website or ironing his choir robe went to Jenny. Sarita was now filled with pleasure and anguish at the prospect of Priest Matthew's reaction to her high heels.

"I joined a self-help group once," Binod said. "We met every Saturday to meditate and talk about self-improvement, but I quit because I didn't have the patience or the humility."

"So?"

"I have a lot of respect for you, for how far you've come in life."

"Everyone in my family thinks I'm an accident waiting to happen," she said.

"You're a risk-taker."

"A proud girl in my village is like a snake that must be tamed before it harms others."

"Tell me about your family," he said, as if he could sense her predicament to want to open up.

Did she eat beef? Did she have sex before marriage? That was her family. She had come to accept that her parents were unable to shake off their simple ways. Even though the caste system was unlawful in the new constitution, her parents were prisoners of fate, as were her older brothers, who defended her one day and called her arrogant the next. She could be a teacher at most, they said, probably because teachers were paid so little, they seemed melancholic and defeated. It was the Bible that gave Sarita the confidence to leave behind a life mired in caste mentality. A life where a lower-caste woman couldn't even step inside the kitchen of anyone above her station. Sarita followed the light to Mary Magdalene, the first to bear witness to the risen Christ. She was so proud that her chosen name was Mary.

"Never mind," she finally said to Binod.

"That answer was worth the wait." He smiled.

The waiter brought their order on an engraved, silver tray. His bow tie seemed odd in this deserted place.

Sarita sipped her coffee without looking at Binod but felt his gaze on her. Each time she laid eyes on him, he wasn't looking at her, but out over the hills, lost in some thought. The top three buttons of his shirt were undone. She noticed a faint scar on his neck, like a birthmark, and she felt a tingle somewhere deep. She reached for the fruitcake and took a bite.

He moved his chair to face her. "We should do this more often," he said. "Look, I tease you because you're so tense all the time."

"You know what takes guts, Binod? Showing this—your sensitive side around your lackeys."

He ran his finger along the table, avoiding her eyes.

"How come you don't have a girlfriend? Waiting for your mom to find you a nice Hindu girl?" she asked.

"How come you don't have a boyfriend? Aren't Christian women supposed to be—"

"Be what?"

He picked his words carefully. "Bold," he said, before adding, "and westernized."

"You can say it. Loose and easy. I know the rumors. Is that why you asked me out? Because I'm bold?"

"You have a mind of your own. I find that attractive."

He placed his hand on top of hers and circled her soft skin with the tip of his finger. Frightened and elated, she drew her hand back.

"I won't eat you," he said.

She felt a rush of blood in her cheeks.

"Do you have siblings?" she asked.

"Only son. I've always had the pressure to be *the* son. The hope. You know what that's like."

"So, you're part of the problem in our country. The sons and only sons." She took out her abridged Simple English Bible and turned to Revelation 3:20. "Read a passage. You won't regret it," she said.

"Seriously? You want to do this now? You know, you will probably have more friends if you make yourself a little less pushy." He grimaced.

"Fine. Let's just snap at each other."

He took the book from her and let it rest in his palm for a moment, as if he was weighing its worth. The golden inscription *The Bible* shone on the cover. He ran his finger along the etched letters, then lightly scratched the soft-leather spine with his thumbnail. He turned the pages and scanned the words. He seemed to be reading more than a few lines.

"What?" she said.

"'I stand at the door, and knock; if a man hears my voice, and opens the door, I will eat with him, and he with me. Whoever brings back a sinner from his lost journey will save his soul from death' . . . Am I a lost soul?" he asked.

"Isn't everyone?"

He leaned closer. "How does a lost soul get salvation?"

"Salvation comes to those who wait," she said, quickly regretting her response. "Why are you stuck in the remittance room, by the way? This is hardly ambitious for a man with a master's in history. Isn't that what you told me?" she asked, impressed by his good English.

"The manager says I'm all show no substance," he said.

"I agree."

They laughed together.

"I wish I could afford college," she said before realizing how much time had passed. She checked her mobile. "I've never been late," she said.

"We're just getting started," he said.

She left her coffee half finished. He paid, and on the way out, he said, "There's something different about you. New shoes?"

A flock of birds unfurled their wings into the beautiful sky.

It started to rain, the first of many monsoon rains. Sarita was drenched. They rode past adjoining brick houses whose ground floors were let out to cafes, bookshops, vegetable shops, bicycle repair shops, barbers, and butchers. The shopkeepers squatted under tin awnings, smoking their cigarettes, staring at the rain and at passersby.

"You're okay?" Binod asked.

The rain came down hard. Binod pulled over by a temple.

"Let's go in and wait this out," he said.

Sarita called the bank on her mobile, but the line was busy. Binod held her hand and led her into the narrow courtyard. They removed their shoes at the entrance. The temple looked as if it had been built in haste, to let stray dogs wander in for a brief shelter from the rain. Were it not for a row of diyas burning in front of Kali's statue, it would have been impossible to navigate in the dark. The only other person in this cave-like room was a bearded beggar stooping for coins that devotees placed at the foot of the goddess Kali. The room permeated with the smell of vermilion powder and the stench of uncollected garbage that wafted from the alley. The beggar grinned at them and walked away.

Binod offered her a clean handkerchief to wipe her face with, but Sarita had one in her own purse. She let her wet hair fall then combed her fingers through it and gently squeezed the end. Then she threw her hair back. He was looking at her. She felt a bit shy, but safe around him, which surprised her. In him there was a hidden capacity to care—she knew it. She wished she could take him to church. They would kneel and pray together. She was now beyond doubt that the church was the guiding force he needed to turn his life around. Everyone needed a sign, and this moment, right now, rain and thunder, was Binod's to seize. Besides, Sarita was slightly disgusted at the state of this temple, like so many others in the city. How ancient it looked compared to her clean, brightly lit church. Though it had only been two years since she had last been in a temple, it felt like her first time in a strange world. She wanted to escape this dismal place and run to her church and fall on her knees before the altar and surrender herself completely to the Lord. She closed her eyes and saw an image in which she swayed her arms in the air . . .

"Sarita." Binod put his hands on her shoulders.

"Sorry," she said.

"No, you look beautiful," he said.

He looked at her cleavage, wet and slightly exposed. She covered it gently with her dupatta. She felt a rush. Their eyes locked. Her lips quivered. He touched her lips with his finger and began kissing them slowly. They kissed like they needed each other right there and then.

Her knees felt weak, and she had no strength to resist. When she realized what she was doing, she pulled herself back with a jolt.

He was breathing loudly. Then without warning, he slid his hand underneath her bra and squeezed her naked breast. "Don't. I don't like that," she said. He gripped her arm with one hand and forced the other hand into her bra again, clumsily trying to grope whatever he could clutch at. "I said, don't," she said and managed to push him away. His eyes, fixed on hers, were trembling. She wasn't sure if she should stay or run, but she stood. The air between them was now sour.

Binod hurried to his motorbike. She sat behind him again but did not wrap her arms around him. The rain had abated. Taxis, tempoos, motorbikes converged upon the street. Sarita felt trapped in a swarm of noise and smoke. She was angry and confused, unable to sort through her feelings. It didn't help that she could smell the mixture of musky cologne and damp sweat emanating from Binod's back. She knew Jesus would forgive her, though in her heart she felt she deserved to be punished so she wouldn't be bold enough to be so reckless again. She tried to fight off the anger she felt at Jesus. He had so much capacity for love, yet he was capable of ruthless tests that Sarita now felt severely victimized by.

The least Binod could do was ask how she was, or something. A yearning to hear his voice grew in her.

"Stop. I want to get off," she said.

He pulled over. "Your mole is disgusting," he said, and without looking at her, he drove away. Sarita took a taxi to work, changed her mind midway, and asked the driver to drop her off at the church.

A woman was sweeping the floor with a baby tied to her back. There was no one else. The marble altar was covered with white cloth on top of which red roses were arranged in several rows surrounded by brass candlesticks. A crucifix hung on a wall behind the altar, and on either side of the crucifix, marble columns struck a gracious pose. Stone-carved angels stood on their cornices looking up at a mural of the sun rising behind Mount Everest.

Sarita knelt with her hands clasped.

"Lord, what do I wait for? My hope is in you," she said. This was not even the sort of thing she could take to confession. Priest Matthew might punish her with silence for months, and if word got out, she would lose every small gain she had worked hard toward. It didn't help that she had enjoyed kissing him. Her pulse had stopped for a moment. Could she have stopped him from groping her? Had she overreacted? She now became resentful of everything—her fate, her life, and especially the sound of broom reeds scraping the floor. She wanted to quarrel with Jesus, but her body, from her head to her toes, filled with infinite sadness.

"Special day?" It was Priest Matthew in a cassock.

He glanced at her high heels. Sarita wasn't going to cry in front of him.

"See me in my office," he said.

She followed him into the room that smelled of stale ink. There was a desk with a computer next to a filing cabinet. A stack of newspapers lay gathering dust on top of the cabinet. He closed the door. Her heart beat faster. She had been in this room only once before, when she had made the confession about desire.

"I need a fresh pair of eyes to tally our expenses," he said. "These are the bills from the last three months. Open the spreadsheet and double-check my numbers." He handed her a file.

He had never let her touch the computer before, and he didn't trust people easily with bills. Sarita didn't know how to use a spreadsheet.

"You can sit on my chair," he said. The leather chair had a towel draped over the headrest. Sarita sat on a plastic chair on the other side of the desk. He rearranged the files in the cabinet and talked about book-keeping issues, lack of funds. The screen saver flashed Jesus offering the eucharist to a girl. Sarita struck a fly on the desk with a rolled news-paper. Priest Matthew looked at her, momentarily distracted by the still-ness of death. He went back to his files, talking about the corruption of mankind, the violence inflicted on the poor. His words floated in the air like apparitions.

∾

Parts of Sarita's suruwal were still damp when she reached the bank. She had finally returned the receptionist's call. She had never been late, had never missed a day of work. She apologized to the waiting customers, who quickly lined up in front of her desk. She wiped her face and hands with a fresh handkerchief and got down to work. Binod and his cronies started talking in whispers. He said something, prompting them to laugh and whistle.

"One moment okay, dai?" Sarita said to a customer. She reached in her purse and took out her cross. She placed it on her desk so that it stared directly back at him. Then she took off her shoes. All day the weight of her body had rested on her poor feet crunched in those high heels. It felt good to let the feet get some air. She even cracked a bone in her toe. She wanted to hurl a shoe at him, let the stiletto stab his face like a dagger, but she had to play smart. She dealt with all her customers, and an hour before closing, stepped into the manager's office.

"It's either them or me," she said. The manager, apparently annoyed by her tardiness earlier, responded immediately, without even listening to what Sarita had to say.

"Your fetish for the church and the Bible should stop at the door, Sarita. Some people are fed up with your Lord this and Jesus that. Do you know that the only complaint we've received in the complaint box is about you and your Bible?"

The transition from hope to weariness in Sarita was swift. She felt exhausted. She was almost about to leave when the manager said, "Sit down. Tell me what you came for. I just had to remind you about that before it escaped me."

Sarita gathered her breath, her courage, and slowly she opened up. The manager listened intently as Sarita told her about the bullying, and in the spur of the moment, the temple incident was laid bare on the table.

To her surprise, the manager appeared sympathetic.

"You are a hard-working employee. I value you," she said, putting her hand on Sarita's. "But you must forget about that."

Of course, Sarita thought.

Her mind wandered back to the month she had joined the bank. All the staff members had gathered in the conference room to watch a video about gender discrimination in the workplace. A woman appeared on the screen and talked monotonously for forty-five minutes about sections and codes in the constitution. Sarita had expected to be educated about different scenarios in which gender discrimination might occur, but the whole ordeal was so boring that most of the employees were chatting or looking at their phones during the screening. Later, a man who supposedly worked in HR but was really the accountant said people with complaints should write their reports on a piece of paper and drop it in the complaint box placed next to the manager's office, in full view of the main section of the bank. Those who dared to walk to the complaint box would no doubt risk being a subject of gossip.

"There was no witness, and we can't control what happens outside our premises," the manager said.

"But there is still the issue of who Binod really is. How many times must I complain to be taken seriously?"

"This is the first time I'm hearing about any kind of harassment. You've complained about the room. A very different matter. Why did you go out with him, knowing the kind of person you claim he is?"

Sarita looked for the right words. "I thought he was sincere," she said.

"Binod is a show-off and he's lazy. I've given him an earful about his tardiness. Write a complaint and put it in the box. I'll take it up with him and speak to HR if necessary."

It sounded like a well-practiced performance. Sarita's forehead creased. Anyone who came into this room was treated with an impressive display of framed certificates on the wall. There was also a photo of the goddess Lakshmi in her resplendent red sari, standing tall on a floating lotus with elephants on either side spraying water at her feet. The ironic symbolism of female power and prosperity wasn't lost on Sarita, nor was the demonstration of piety given the castigation earlier. "With due respect, madam, your lectures to Binod haven't really worked. This is about a woman's safety," she said.

The manager raised her eyebrow, seemingly struck by Sarita's boldness or by the truthfulness of those words. She then put her hand on her chin and sat like that for a while. She asked Sarita to go back to her desk and return in half an hour.

When Sarita opened the door, she found Binod near the water cooler outside the manager's office. She looked him in the eye for a second and kept walking.

"We need to talk," he said. She ignored him. He followed her into the remittance room and sat behind her even after everyone had left.

"This is what I can do," the manager said when Sarita returned to her office. "I'll remove them from that room."

Sarita wasn't sure she heard this correctly.

"The Bhaktapur branch is looking for an administrative assistant. I can send Binod there. The other two I'll figure something out."

Sarita had been hopeful but unprepared for this turnaround.

"Can I ask what made you change your mind?" she said. She had no expectation that anything would actually get done.

"There's something about you, Sarita, that is utterly earnest. I don't doubt that Binod mistreated you. For your own well-being, a formal investigation will drag unnecessarily into a long scandal, and I would not recommend it. You call it bullying, they will call it casual fun. We are not equipped to discern the difference, especially with no witnesses. A smarter way to deal with him would be to send him off. The Bhakta-pur branch with its two-hour daily commute will be a good wake-up call for him. It's a demotion. I've been fed up with his recklessness, anyway."

We meet our destiny on the path we're not supposed to take, Sarita had heard. Did she have to go through this trial for something to finally move in her favor? Before she left the office, the manager said thank you—"for bringing this to my attention."

Sarita felt a lightness in her heart. She smiled.

In the parking lot, Binod was sitting on his bike, staring ahead. He revved up the engine when he saw her.

"Hi, look, I'm sorry. Can we talk?" he said. But she kept walking, keeping her expression as grave as she could. He slowly circled the bike around her and exited the lot. Sarita didn't want to read too much into that. With a touch of vindication and relief, she held the cross in her purse, and soon she was lost in the crowded street. A swelling knot of fear tickled through her bones. Would Binod lash out at her? She had

heard enough about such violence and hate, but she couldn't bear thinking about it.

"The saddest part is that my betrayal didn't come from an enemy,
from Binod, or Priest Matthew. It came from you, my Lord. But I know
in every trial lies a blessing. You have shown me a blessing. Please help
me find the strength," she said as her feet invariably moved in the direction of the church.

Haircut and Massage

It was quite early in the morning, but Krishna's first thoughts were about Iqbal, his barber. Though his wife was nagging him, he left the house and walked to the salon like there was no time to lose.

The barber was standing on the pavement, smoking tobacco leaf.

"Welcome, hazur, welcome." He smiled. He stubbed the beedi between his fingers and led Krishna through the curtain into the clean, brightly lit salon—Good-Day Haircut. Big mirrors lined the walls; next to each mirror was a poster of a Bollywood star.

Iqbal was from the southern plains of Nepal, a migrant in the city of Kathmandu. He kept a carefully trimmed pencil mustache, put a faint touch of kohl around his eyes, and combed back his sleek hair. The checkered cloth that he draped around his waist, with the crisp white shirt that hung on his dark skin, gave him the look of a bygone actor from a Hindi film. While he cut Krishna's hair, he was mostly silent, as if he secretly cried for chopping off hair that wasn't his, but when he spoke, he delivered words like musical notes—high-pitched for emphasis and long inflections when he was particularly lyrical. Krishna often complimented him for his poetic voice and the answers never failed to impress. He would say things like, "What can I do, hazur? My heart is still in the rice fields of my village, long left behind. If my voice is lush, it is because my heart speaks in the colors of the green fields and the tall grass."

Krishna sat on his favorite chair, the one with a soft, red cushion seat. After the white cloth was draped around his shoulders and the string tied behind his back, he closed his eyes.

"You left your wife back in the village, no, Iqbal?" Krishna asked, as strands of hair fell on the white cloth.

"My begum has laid her nest in my heart," Iqbal said. "All I have to do is listen to my heartbeat. Like they say, hazur, our love finds expression in small gestures with grand meanings."

After the haircut, the barber gently pressed Krishna's temples and forehead; then, without asking, one by one, he undid Krishna's top three buttons and let his fingers slide under the shirt. He kneaded the skin, massaging, pressing, working his way slowly to the curve of the shoulders. Krishna's skin quivered at the touch, and in a voice barely audible, he mumbled, "Enough, enough."

"As you wish," the barber said and expertly cracked Krishna's neck bones and held up a mirror behind him.

Krishna gave him a hundred and twenty rupees—the twenty, an unusually big amount—as a tip. When he stepped out of the salon, he had a soft smile on his face, and he remembered to button his shirt as he passed by the sweet shop. The shopkeeper, wearing a dirty undershirt, stirred a huge cauldron where the flower-pattern jeris swam in hot oil. The jeri's sugary syrup trickled down your chin when you bit into it. "This time don't forget to pick up sweets and vegetables on your way back. Please!" Krishna's wife had said, but after the massage and tip, he could barely afford any.

"Jeris?" his daughter asked as soon as he got home. She lay in bed, listening to music on her headphones.

"Later, okay?" Krishna said.

Nani rolled her eyes and blew a curl of hair that fell to her nose.

In the kitchen, Krishna separated water from the rice.

"That barber, Iqbal, I feel sad for him. Do you know he goes home only once a year to meet his family?" he said to his wife as the water drained in the sink.

"I'm making dal and spinach again. Nothing else." Sabitri stirred the lentils and put a drop on her palm to taste the salt. "Go take your bath. I don't want your hair messing up my kitchen."

"Next time I won't tip him so much," Krishna said. "Don't get angry."

"Always one excuse or another," Sabitri said and threw a bunch of spinach in the hot oil.

At work the next day, Krishna talked to a colleague about the blissful effects of a haircut and a shoulder massage.

The colleague looked up from behind a heap of files.

"You only go for the shoulders?" he said. "I do the whole body and leg routine every month. Really, since I have been doing that, my life has changed, I tell you."

"Is that so?"

"Call him at home. They come for a few extra rupees."

A few days later, upon Krishna's request, Iqbal came to his house, carrying a wooden box full of scissors, a small mirror, and an assortment of oils and powders. He offered a salaam to Krishna at the door, puffing on the inevitable tendu leaf that was a part of his personality.

"Tell him he can't smoke that thing here. Don't know why you had to bring him home," Sabitri muttered.

"Why don't you make a cup of tea for him now, please." Krishna nudged her, then led the barber to the veranda, where he had spread out a mattress. "I hope this is not inconvenient for you. We will skip the haircut today. But I want you to do a good massage on me. Let me also see what this 'body massage' is all about," he said, trying a laugh.

Sabitri brought tea in a china cup for Krishna, and in a steel tumbler for Iqbal. She put the barber's cup a few steps from him. After she left, Krishna offered his guest the china cup.

"Whatever you wish, hazur," the barber replied and poured his tea in the saucer, blew on it, and took a sip, making a long, slurpy sound.

"Take off your shirt, hazur," he said after finishing his tea.

For some reason, Krishna felt shy. He unbuttoned his shirt and put it on the side. To make up for his receding hairline, his chest was generously endowed with hair, which made him all the more self-conscious. Iqbal sat on his haunches, combing his pencil mustache and stealing furtive glances at Krishna, his kohl glistening in the afternoon sun. After taking off the religious thread that hung on his shoulders, Krishna lay with his face down.

Little drops of oil fell on his back, and slowly, the barber massaged him. How good it felt: the afternoon sun, the chirping of birds on nearby trees, the warm oil. Iqbal turned into a skillful masseur. He bunched

his fists and ran them up and down Krishna's back, and along the way,
quite playfully, squeezed the folds of his client's skin.

"What are you doing?" Krishna asked, giggling, but Iqbal only responded with his long fingers, now supple, massaging the curves, feeling out the shapes and contours of Krishna's body. Slowly the fingers
reached down and pulled Krishna's cotton trousers just an inch below
his waist and poured teasing drops of oil on the tip of his buttocks.

"Enough," Krishna said, suddenly sitting up. The oil dripped like a
tiny stream under his trousers. Krishna looked around to see if his wife
or daughter were watching.

"Hazur, is anything the problem?" Iqbal asked.

"No, no."

"Should I be gentler?"

"No, that's not it."

"Your skin is so soft, hazur. My bare hands sink into it so gracefully."

Krishna smiled. He lay down again, this time with his face up and
eyes closed.

The drops of oil trickled on his stomach, and the fingers moved
slower, gentler. Krishna lay captive as Iqbal kneaded his skin as a snake
charmer might play with a cobra: exciting it and taming it at the same
time, and the long fingers stole away bits of shyness hiding in every pore
of Krishna's skin. Before he knew it, the middle-aged man was moaning.
He opened his eyes, pushed Iqbal's hands away, and sat up. His heart
was knocking on his chest.

"Hazur?"

Krishna picked up his shirt and took out a crumpled hundred-rupee
note. He nervously clutched the note in Iqbal's palm.

"Will I have the service of attending to your hair soon?"

"We'll see. You can go now," Krishna said and left the veranda.

That night, in bed, he turned this way and that. Sabitri was softly
snoring, her back to him.

◦~◦

A year ago, Krishna had won an office lottery, a free overnight stay for
two at a hill resort, a few hours from Kathmandu.

"Take the children, they will enjoy the scenery," Sabitri had said. Nani responded with a "No way," but Babu, their son, really wanted to go. "Father has never taken me anywhere," he said. Then Nani started grumbling—if Babu was going, why couldn't she go, too? They got into a fight with their mother; at the end they were packed off to a relative's house for the night, and it was Krishna and his wife who took the long bus journey out to the hills. They had their free meal in an empty restaurant, then sat looking out the window. Sabitri complained about how Krishna was not being the dominating father he needed to be. Nani showed no respect to her elders.

"Why do you always see the negative?" Krishna said.

"Raising a daughter is not like drinking water. It requires thought, some control. She doesn't listen to me because you don't say a thing to her."

"What do you want me to do?"

"Be a father. Be a man. Daughters should be allotted a measured amount of love, so they don't feel deprived when they go to a new house."

"What new house? She's just a teenager."

Sabitri sighed. "What is our room number?" she said.

In room 206, Krishna lay in bed, his arm over his head. Sabitri rested against the bed post, knitting a sweater. Just as she was measuring the length of the sweater on his arm, he turned, and started kissing her palm, her wrist, her elbow.

"Wait," she said. The wool got entangled in his hand. She laughed. He pinched her. She gave him a mean look. He threw the half-knit sweater away, grabbed her, and kissed her neck.

"Slowly," she said.

"It's been so long."

"Still."

Afterward they lay side by side, staring at the ceiling. Sabitri hated the hotel pillows. They were too big, too soft. Why hadn't they brought their own pillows from home? Why were they so poor at planning things?

"Let's sleep," Krishna said and turned around. There was a time when his wife's eyes traveled so delicately over his body, when her fingers ran so playfully across his lips, when her voice on the phone left him with no choice but to sneak out of work and come running home. After the first child was born, though, something changed in Sabitri, and she began a lifelong affair with discontent. It was as if their bedroom had turned overnight into a stale and musty room where Sabitri aired daily grievances about cooking and cleaning, and Krishna listened dutifully, staring vacantly at the wall, offering to help when he could, fully knowing that he would never know how to cure all her sufferings.

~

A week after the massage, Iqbal's touch rippled in Krishna's body, all day long. The barber had begun to engage his mind to a degree that made him scared and uncomfortable, but he wasn't sure what to do about such thoughts. At work, he tried to concentrate on the bills and memos piling up on his desk, but at the merest thought of the barber, he would feel a sensation in his groin and his heart would beat faster. Krishna would then try to divert his mind by silently reciting slokas from the Bhagavad Gita in an effort to make sense of sensations he had no control over.

"What is the matter with you? Are you not feeling well?" his wife asked one evening.

"I'm all right," he said and looked away.

She was squatting, mopping the floor with a piece of rag. "You forgot to buy beetroot on your way from work. Go now, I have to cook soon," she said, wiping the sweat off her forehead with her finger.

"When will a man have some peace?" Krishna grumbled on his way to the market, and after some thought, he dropped in to see Iqbal, but the salon was closed. Krishna knocked, but there was no response. He peeped through a little crack and knocked louder.

"Hazur." Iqbal was on the other side of the road, watching. He walked toward Krishna with a smile and pushed the doors open.

"Salaam, hazur, you haven't paid me a visit in a while. Even my bare walls echo with your absence. See how they light up now," Iqbal said and turned on the tube lights, which showered the salon with brightness. "You stopped the massage suddenly the other day. I hope it did not reflect my service. Were you unhappy, hazur?"

"No, no. Why would I be unhappy with you? In fact, I was thinking maybe we could resume the massage. You see, I am having a little pain around my shoulders."

"Shoulder massage, hazur?"

"We can do body, if you want."

"What do *you* want?" Iqbal said.

"Okay, body. If you don't mind."

"How can I mind, hazur? Take off your shirt."

"Here?" Krishna said. A boy was sweeping the floor. Krishna did not notice when this boy had come in.

The barber said something to the boy, who threw away the broom, jiggled his hips, whistled a filmy tune, and ran out.

Krishna took off his shirt and Iqbal hung it on a peg.

"You enjoy doing this, Iqbal?" Krishna asked.

"Hazur, the art of massage has been passed down in my family for generations. It is said that my great-great-grandfather was a private masseur to a very rich landlord in the village who had one masseur for his left arm, one for his right arm, one for the head, one for just the legs, and so on. When my ancestor placed his hand on the landlord's arm, the great man cried with joy. All the other masseurs were immediately fired, and my great-great-great grandfather . . ."

"Great-great-great or just great-great?" Krishna teased him.

"You're too funny, hazur," Iqbal said. "Anyhow," he continued, "my great-great grandfather became the man's designated, one and only . . . I'll make sure you're comfortable."

He took out a round cushion from a drawer and put it on the wooden panel. "Place your head here."

Eyes closed, Krishna felt the same sensation again. It was as if the barber was inviting him into another world, a world that had space for only the two of them. When the barber touched the small of his back, Krishna was breathing hard, as if snatching at the last breaths of his life.

"Hazur?"

He was holding the barber's hand.

"Don't you wish to continue?" Iqbal asked.

"That's enough." Krishna quickly withdrew his hand. He put on his shirt, left every rupee and paisa he had on the counter, and walked out. He couldn't hear if Iqbal was calling him back or not.

He went straight to a temple and sat cross-legged, folding his palms and closing his eyes before Kali, the blue goddess. The priest appeared from behind and dabbed red vermilion powder on the goddess's forehead. "Stepped inside for a change?" he said, but Krishna pretended not to hear him. When he reached home, he could not remember where he left the vegetable packet. Despite the children's frantic protests at dinner, Sabitri only served rice and pickles. She ate quickly and left the kitchen, forcing her husband to clean the plates.

That night, the table fan rotated with a louder grunt as if it were making fun of him.

"Is something wrong with you?" Sabitri asked, her voice soaked with sleep.

"No, no. Go back to sleep," Krishna said.

"You're tossing and turning. Don't think I don't know what's going on."

"What?"

"You seem lost these days. Is something the matter?"

For a moment he wondered if he should tell her. That would ease his burden. Husbands and wives talked about such things, after all.

"Nani's future," he said.

She turned around. "What?"

"She does well in school. Why should we weigh her down with our doubts, our objections, our suspicions? Why?"

"What is the matter with you?"

He drew a long breath.

Sabitri placed a hand on his shoulder. "Sita didi saw her with a boy outside school the other day," she said. "He was smoking god-knows-what and had tattoos on his arm. Nani rode on a motorcycle with that hooligan. What will people say? What if they see her roaming with such types? We are simple, middle-class people."

He kept quiet.

"Just remember that it only takes a whiff of scandal for the stench to spread. People will notice."

He did not respond, and after a while, she covered her head with the quilt.

He clutched the bedsheet with his clammy palms, struggling with all kinds of thoughts. What was happening to him? Where did these thoughts come from? He had never considered the possibility of being attracted to a man before. He was disgusted by the thought alone.

Krishna was back at the salon the next morning. Iqbal was cutting someone else's hair, so Krishna had to wait on a bench. Iqbal told his customer a joke about the Mogul emperor Akbar and they both laughed heartily. Krishna looked away.

The haircut was followed by a head massage and the customer did not leave before showering his appreciation with a tidy tip. Iqbal bowed and offered his salaam to the customer. Then he dusted off the white cloth and greeted Krishna.

"Hazur, I've been thinking about you," Iqbal said. "You left abruptly again. Seems like my service has not met your standards lately. You know, hazur, a cook can prepare the best cuisine by sprinkling all the spices of nature, but if he forgets the salt, it is an insult to the guest's taste buds. Perhaps, I might have unknowingly insulted the high standards I reserve for you. Allow me to be gentler this time."

Krishna looked around. There was no one else in the salon. He kept his voice down. "Don't think I don't know your tricks," he said.

"Hazur?"

"You manipulate your customers. After all these months, it took me one moment to realize what you're up to. You make people take off their shirts and expose them to ways not proper in this town. This is why people say outsiders like you are polluting our home."

The barber's veins stood out on his forehead.

"Hazur?"

"This is all very filthy."

"Sir, you're insulting my trade," Iqbal said.

"What right did you have to play with my body like that? Huh?"

Iqbal took a few steps forward, prompting Krishna to step out. On the pavement, loud enough for passersby to hear, Iqbal shouted, "In all of history, fools have always mistaken art for trickery."

Krishna had never been so humiliated. He had to escape immediately. As he walked down the street, shaking with a mixture of fear and loathing, he suddenly saw Sabitri.

"Listen!" she shouted. She stood with a bag of vegetables in front of a stall. "Why are you walking so fast?" she asked.

"Oh, you are here?"

"Where did you disappear all morning? My whole mood is spoiled. This vegetable market is a competition for cheats."

"Let's go home. I'm really tired," he said.

"We need squash. Come with me and carry the bags. What are you doing roaming around?"

"Nothing," Krishna said.

"You are starting to smell like a barber. It's that attar smell, permanently stuck in your shirt. Did you visit that fellow again?

"What are you talking about?"

"I saw you walking out of his shop."

Krishna slowed down his steps, averting her glances, afraid of what might be uncovered if those glances were acknowledged. He paused before a puddle, trying to steady himself against the emotions beating against his chest savagely. One got used to stepping on dry potholes in Kathmandu, though puddles always posed a challenge depending on their depth and girth. This one was a mini crater.

"Hold my hand," Sabitri said, hitching up her sari to her knees. A man behind Krishna told him to hurry up.

"What are you waiting for? Contemplating suicide?" Sabitri's impatient voice was raised a few notches. There were many thoughts in Krishna's mind. Did she suspect something? Was it possible for Sabitri to ever imagine anything in the realm of what was going on with him?

"Hurry up, Baba," she said.

In the midst of these thoughts, Sabitri extended her hand toward him. As he held it, he felt her firm grip, the grip of his wife of years. Of generations and centuries. On the other side of the puddle, his sandals slightly wet, Krishna followed his wife to the vegetable market.

Student Visa

The morning of the interview, I spend more time in front of the mirror than usual. The black coat goes well with the white shirt. I add a touch of je ne sais quoi with a bowtie, shine my hair with Brylcreem.

"Wear your father's tie instead of that butterfly," Mother says. She walks nervously between the kitchen and the living room, carrying a plate of alu-chiura, urging me to eat something, but the uneasy grumblings in my stomach haven't stopped tormenting me.

"This butterfly is going to soar, Ama," I say.

Mother sighs, half-convinced.

"God willing, Sanjay is going to America, Muwa. Far, far away!" she says to Granny, who sits on a string cot pushed against the wall in the corner. Granny's tiny feet dangle high above the floor, and she sways gently, grunting and mumbling to herself.

Meanwhile Father returns from his morning walk with Bhandari uncle, our neighbor. Unlike Father, who goes for his walks in a regular cotton shirt, cotton trousers, and rubber slippers, Bhandari uncle wears a tracksuit with a pair of "authentic" Nike sneakers that his brother sent from California. I checked—they're actually made in China. When his brother calls, Bhandari uncle speaks loudly on his mobile lest anyone forget that his brother indeed lives in California.

"Going to America, mister?" Bhandari uncle says. He sits on one of our cushioned chairs.

"Let's pass this visa interview first," I say.

"Give him your blessings, dai," says Mother, coming into the room carrying cups of tea.

"One must be an exceptional candidate to get the visa," Bhandari uncle says.

Father sits on a nylon stool, cracking the bones of his toes. "I am not worried," he says. "My son is fluent in English, so no one can question his intelligence. And let's not forget—he has earned a scholarship . . . tell uncle the name of this scholarship."

"It's called the minority scholarship," I say. "For international students."

"These foreigners have a soft spot for Nepal," Bhandari uncle says.

"It only covers fifty percent of tuition. They'll increase it after a year," Father says.

"Americans are shrewd," says Bhandari uncle and sips his tea. "They want us to study in their colleges. Then work for cheaper salaries than the Whites. And listen, learn to drive as soon as you get there. No one walks in America." He turns to Father. "In California, you get arrested for walking on the highway," he says.

"Only for jaywalking," I add.

Father turns to Bhandari uncle, pointing at me with a flick of his eyebrows. "Fully prepared," he says and smiles. "Tell uncle what jaywalking means. We old men don't understand your American words."

"Jaywalking? It just means walking without following rules," I say. Bhandari uncle takes out his mobile from its leather case. He wipes the phone with his sleeve and punches numbers with one finger.

"My six-year-old nephew wanted to FaceTime, but it's almost midnight there," Bhandari uncle finally says. He keeps looking at the phone, prompting Father to ask if he got an important call. Bhandari uncle shakes his head.

"Speaking of rules, Nepal has become the lawless wonder of the world," Father says. He unfolds a crumpled tabloid. "Water-pump scam! These politicians are sucking us dry. After Sanjay settles in America we will eventually follow."

From her room, Mother brings a crisp handkerchief sprayed with a dash of Old Spice. She folds the handkerchief and puts it in my pocket.

She also picks out a loose thread from my coat. "Why don't you relax?" I tell her. Shaking her head, she goes back to the kitchen.

"By the way, what is the name of that young fellow from your office?" Bhandari uncle asks Father, putting his phone back in its leather case. "Shrestha's cousin. Is it true he slid his toe through the door and got the promotion you wanted?"

Father takes off his shirt and rolls it into a bundle. The collar is black on the inside. He wipes his neck with the shirt. "The bastard had connections. There's a rumor that Shrestha went up to the minister, greasing every palm along the way."

"Shrestha is smart that way."

"A corrupt swine. That is what he is. I am happy that my son is going to a country where success is based on merit."

"Merit alone won't take you far. Even in America, the Whites rule for a reason. You've always been too naive, Karki," Bhandari uncle says. "He who is thirsty needs to find the spring."

"I have a master's in electrical engineering."

"Which we hang on a wall to hide a crack," Mother says. "The last time I checked, it brought no extra money." She is now sitting at the dining table, removing stems from spinach leaves. The table is set in one corner of the crammed living room.

No one talks for a while.

"There is no prospect for technocrats in our government, Karki. How often have I told you to get a job in the private sector? Be a consultant."

"We have invested all our savings in Sanjay's education. This American school has wiped us out," Mother says. "If destiny is fair, even Muwa will live the last years of her life in good health."

"Dog shit," Granny says, bunching her fist. Bhandari uncle laughs. Mother gives Father a quick glance. I walk over and kneel beside Granny. She places her trembling hand on mine. "Go and play," she says. I give her arm a gentle rub, which brings sleep to her eyes.

"Listen," Bhandari uncle says to me. "Take my brother's name at the interview. Tell them he's ready to sponsor you. Make something up. They won't find out."

Father looks uneasily at me.

"It doesn't work like that, uncle," I say. "Let's not go that far. Besides, they might ask for a sponsor letter."

Bhandari uncle hands father a business card from his wallet. "You may eat what you want, but you wear for others. It's called networking," he says, getting up to leave. Mother asks what's the hurry and if he would sit for another cup of tea.

"Nothing less than goat meat for the celebration," he says with a laugh. Father buttons up a fresh shirt and accompanies him out.

I gently pry away Granny's fingers, which are clasped around my wrist. I get up, straighten my coat. When Father returns, he slips the business card in my pocket. "Just in case," he says, and I don't want to argue. He also puts a five-hundred-rupee bill in my hand for the taxi. "Don't take the tempoo and reach there smelling of dust," he says.

From the kitchen, Mother brings a tray filled with wick lamps and circles it in front of my face. I bow my head for blessings, then touch Granny's feet, which are bunched together, like a tiny sack of wrinkles. She opens her eyes and runs her fingers over my face, mumbling a prayer for every part of me she touches. "Going to school?" she asks.

I hesitate to answer, but Mother says, "Far away."

"Check all your documents," Father says, which I do. When Mother embraces me, I can feel her beating heart. "Ama, it's okay," I tell her.

"Go on, you'll be late," she says, turning away, as if I'm leaving for America at that very moment.

In the alley, Father walks ahead of me. Before I get into a taxi, he pats my shoulder. "No need to worry too much; we are already proud of you," he says.

"Of course, Baba, I know," I say.

～

The taxi driver is napping in the back seat. The ripped seat is covered with sweat. He seems bitter for having to wake up from his daydream. As he drives through the crowded street, I look out at the twisted electric wires, looped around poles and trees, entangled in knots, hanging between houses that are gray with dust. We pass by the marble soda shop. The marble rattles in the bottle when you drink the fizzy soda that comes in orange and blue. I still remember—when I turned six, my father had taught me how to press down the marble with my thumb to pop open the bottle, something I'd been waiting to do for a whole year. It was a rainy day. Mother, Father, Granny, and I stood under the awning of the soda shop. Those were the days when Granny could still walk with a stooped back. I pushed the marble with a finger, prompting the fizz to rise and the marble to rattle in the dent of the neck. "Drink, drink," Mother had said, laughing, making me drink straight from the bottle. Our drinks savored, we walked back in the rain, all of us huddled under a giant umbrella. I now regret not taking pictures of such moments to take with me to America.

"Hundred rupees in the pocket. Should I save that for petrol or potato, you tell me?" the driver asks. A frayed toothbrush hangs from a string tied to the rearview mirror. He looks at me. "American visa means there's too much luck crammed in your forehead," he says.

"I've been waiting for this day since I was a kid."

"How so?"

"It's the kind of education you get at the American School," I say. "I was on the basketball team. I played guitar in the school rock band. We even had American teachers. You know what our school motto was? Live for Humanity, Lead for Nepal. But they actually teach you to look at Nepal through rose-tinted glasses, like foreigners. Every year, there's a news flash in the school to announce who among the graduates got the visa. It's like winning the lottery. Almost everyone applies."

"Isn't that the school behind the big walls? Expensive?"

"Let's just say that at some point, my parents' dreams became my own."

"Everything in life is luck. You have it or you don't."

"Then, of course, the never-ending application process. I've spent hours in the library. Guess how much it costs to apply to a college? Just to apply?"

"Tell me."

"Fifteen thousand."

The man smiles in wonder.

"I need this, brother. I need this badly," I say.

The driver drums his fingers on the steering wheel, looking at me every now and then through the mirror. I can't believe I expressed my deepest thoughts and worries to a stranger in a taxi. Maybe it's the realization that I could be in Utah in two months.

Thankful for the driver's silence for the rest of the ride, I open my folder and pull out a document with prospective questions to brush up on some key points. When we reach the embassy, the man insists he has no change. He owes me two hundred rupees. He says, "Just step out of the taxi. I'll park by the curb and see if the tea seller can give us a change for five hundred." I'm skeptical. As soon as I'm out of the cab, he drives off, yelling a seven-generation curse. I knew it. Fucker. I have no time for regrets. I look at my watch and walk to the main gate.

The magnificent embassy, with enormous walls and high-tech gadgets on the roof, towers over the street like a twenty-first-century mountain. Most passersby stop briefly to look at it before moving on. There's a slow-moving line of visa applicants that stretches all the way to the end of the wall. A kind-looking woman lets me sneak in front, prompting a chorus of complaints, but we hold back from breaking into an argument, awed as we are by the building's grandiosity.

After walking through a scanner and leaving our phones in a basket, we are let in. The first thing I notice is the absolute silence. The traffic noise cannot reach this far. In the air-conditioned waiting room, our footprints dissolve in the carpet. President Trump's smiling portrait hangs on the wall. This is his territory.

The visa applicants are dressed in their finest—men in suits, women weighed down by jewelry. Two big-chested Nepali security guards walk their Alsatians that seem capable of sniffing out those who twitch and fret too much. The air is filled with nervous murmurs. People share notes of what the Americans might throw at us. When their names are called out from a speaker on the wall, the applicants proceed to the interview booths, their shoulders stooped with worry.

The man sitting next to me nudges me with his elbow.

"Final destination?" he whispers. Three stone-embedded rings decorate his pudgy fingers, and his forehead is smeared with tika.

"Utah."

"Big city?"

"Utah is a state. It became the forty-fifth state on January 4, 1896."

He nods, assessing my face. "You'll get it," he says. "My case is more complicated. I need a tourist visa." He doesn't stop talking. There are questions and comments spewing from his mouth, and I try hard to block him out.

My father would buy me these books when I was small, about NASA, black holes, the ABCs of quantum physics, you name it. "Light travels in straight lines into our eyes—all you need to do is open those eyes, Sanjay," he would say, eager to pass on his love of science to his son, and the hope that I would someday fulfill his desire to study in an American university. Once upon a time it was the Greeks, then Romans and Arabs. Now, America was at the center around whose orbit the rest of the world circled. Mother, who questioned Baba's motives initially, was soon won over. Who wouldn't want to live in such a country of boundless optimism and progress? Talking about hardships together will make those hardships more tolerable, they say, so Baba and Ama would talk late into the night about the wonders of dishwashers and dryers. Eventually, Ama became the torchbearer of our collective dreams, bending over a sewing machine that took up space in the corner of their bedroom, its rhythmic sound filling the silence of our evenings while she stitched pillow covers and tablecloths that she sold at neighboring shops for a handsome price, so she could send her son to an American school. America was a country, she would say, where even a boxer with an aggressive haircut (Mr. T) could be rich and famous. Of course, they were disappointed by my inclination toward literature, but it was better to drive an unremarkable car than to have never driven at all.

Most people who return from the interview complain that the interviewer is a monster—too tough. The few lucky ones walk back with their chins up, generating looks of awe. They are asked to wait while the declined lot is escorted out in a single file. I try to revise key facts, but just as you'd expect, I draw a blank—is the official vessel of Utah the

Dutch oven or the Danish oven? What if I mix up the two? I take out Bhandari uncle's card, run my fingers over the glossy letters:

Eastern Handicrafts and Millennium Entrepreneurs. 1515 Dwight St., San Diego, California 92182. We Mean Business!

"Impossible," says the tourist-visa man, who had been called upon when I was lost in my thoughts. "Take my advice, go back home," he says as he is escorted out by the guard.

When my name is announced, I take a deep breath and walk to the booth with a smile.

A glass partition separates the interviewer from me. She looks like a Nepali. In fact, the brass nameplate on her desk confirms it: Julie Pokhrel. A miniature American flag is pinned to her coat.

"How're you doing this morning?" She speaks into a thin mike in a voice that booms with an American twang. Behind her, a stars and stripes flag covers the wall.

"Fine, thank you, madam," I say, taking my seat, but the mike doesn't catch my voice, so I say it again, and squeeze my folder through a small hole in the glass. The air-conditioning is turned very high.

"Why Utah?" She looks at me over the rim of her rectangular glasses.

I clear my throat.

"Madam, two reasons. First of all, your great country is the melting pot of the world. Its greatness lies in stirring hope in the hearts of those who dare to dream."

She wets her thumb, leafing through my documents, then holds a sheet of my transcript against the light.

"Go on," she says.

"Madam, the second reason is that I may be only one among millions, but through hard work, I aim to convert my own little dream into reality, thereby not only building the foundation of my own life, but contributing to the progress of Nepal upon my return."

"Don't you think Nepal needs young people like you? Now, more than ever?"

"Young people with world-class education who can return to make a true difference. Like Socrates said, 'Education is the kindling of a flame.'" My palms start to sweat. Could it be Plato who said that?

"Your TOEFL score is not as good as your grades."

"As you well know, the famous quote by ex-president George W. Bush: 'America is the land of the second chance—and when the gates of promise open, the path ahead should lead to a better life.'"

She twiddles a pen in her fingers.

"You didn't answer my question. Why Utah? It's not the most popular destination."

Truth was, I had a carefully tiered choice of schools with Utah State University as my "throw things in the wall and see what sticks" option; they ended up giving me the best funding.

"Madam, besides being the birthplace of Terry Tempest Williams, one of my favorite writers, Utah, as you know, is also the home of the Jazz. Big fan."

"Is that so?"

"I've read about their history and know the names of all their legends. Boozer, Stockton, Maloné."

"Wait, did you just say Maloné?" She leans back in her chair and laughs. The laughter booms out from the mike. She bends closer until her nose almost presses against the glass. "Malone. Let the *o* swell."

"Malone," I repeat.

"You want to be American right here, right now, don't you?" When she says that, her accent suddenly slips into Nepali.

I smile. She avoids my eyes.

"Your scholarship is so small. Who'll pay for your education?"

"My parents are very supportive, madam. As is evidenced in the papers," I say and point to the documents declaring Father's savings and the valuation of Mother's jewelry. "In fact, my mother is ready to sell her wedding jewelry." The last line is perhaps uncalled for, but I take the chance because she's Nepali. She doesn't flinch.

"English major, huh? Who's your favorite author?"

"Next to Ms. Williams, the great Maya Angelou, ma'am."

"Seeing as you are a man of quotes, can you recite something she wrote?"

I look at the ceiling. Of course, I draw a blank. I had it memorized down pat.

"Fire, a fire burns in my mind. Do you dare to leave me, I decry. Lover of eyes, don't steal my light. Tear open this heart of mine. Perhaps then you will change your mind."

It's a mangled translated excerpt of "Muna Madan" by Devkota.

"That's good," she says, a smile curled around her lips, not realizing who was fooling whom.

Moments of silence pass between us. The suspense is unbearable.

"Madam, the theme of the poem is mourning, which the poet wonderfully illustrates with . . ."

"Got it," she says. "This is not an English exam."

I give a smile-shrug combination.

She gets up from her chair unexpectedly and walks to a vending machine that looks like a cutting-edge fridge from the future. She puts in a dollar bill and the machine clinks, clanks, spits out a chilled coffee bottle. She tilts her head and takes a sip. The Starbucks logo is enchanting. We only have Star Coffee with a deceivingly similar logo in Kathmandu. She walks back, the bottle in her hand, her gaze fixed on my passport.

A second before she slams the passport with a stamp, I slide the business card to her in a fit of nervousness.

She looks at it, turns it over.

"As a safety net, I also have relatives willing to sponsor me."

"Letter?"

"I don't have it with me at this moment, but I could get it, madam."

She sits down, disappointed. "Sanjay," she says. "I was almost going to approve your visa. Even though your scholarship barely meets the threshold, you sound sincere and smart. But you just shot yourself in the foot. If you claim something, you must prove it with appropriate documents. And you were not even *required* to show sponsorship. I must reject this application. Better luck next time."

She stamps the word DENIED.

My mouth goes dry. "Madam, madam," I try, but no words come out of me, trapped as they are in my chest.

"Sorry." She slides the card back. "I'm just following the rules."

A voice explodes from deep within me. "I need to talk to a *real* American," I shout.

She presses a buzzer, not a hint of emotion in her face. A security guard takes me aside to the long line that is filing out like children expelled from class.

$\sim$

The dust on the road at once ages my black shoes. I walk and keep walking, stumbling into various attempts at explanations of what just happened.

"Where to?" a man asks as his motorbike sputters to a halt. He has a little girl in front and a boy behind him. A stack of iron rods is harnessed to the carrier, leaving barely any space for an extra person.

"Visa reject? Get on. You're not the first. We ride this way every Saturday."

I sit behind the boy. A coarse smell reeks from a jute satchel strapped to his shoulder.

"Where to?" the man asks.

"Dillibazar."

"I'll drop you off near Thamel." He throttles the accelerator, causing the pipes to clatter.

A few minutes later, the boy says, "Would you like to sample our nail cutters?"

"Show uncle some varieties," says the man, whose helmet bounces every time the motorbike hits a pothole. The boy takes out several nail cutters from his satchel, each one a different color and size, and holds them like a row of cards.

"I know you have just returned from a bad interview. But you can chip away the old for the new. How many will you take today?" the boy says.

I feel like smiling. "A shop on two wheels?" I ask.

"I'll throw in a pocket mirror if you buy all five," the boy says.

"I'll take the blue."

He puts it into my coat pocket.

"What are these pipes for?" I ask.

"We are helping build a community school near Thankot," the father says. "Voluntary work, once a week. Company provides material. We move these parts and set them up. You may have read about the school: Ganatantra Bright Future, the first rural school in the district with plans to use computers in every classroom. A 'smart' school!"

I don't respond.

"A tall ambition, but things are moving ahead with everyone's support. Donors, community members, even the government has stepped up."

There was this school trip I'll never forget: we had gone to Panauti for an environmental awareness class. A basket-weaving exhibit by local Newari women was organized for us, the lesson being that the reed baskets were more environmentally friendly than factory-made synthetic material—never mind that all the students were busy playing pranks, drinking Frooti out of Tetra Paks, distributing plastic-wrapped candy to the village kids. I felt so bad, I snuck out during a shopping excursion and sat with the women, who taught me how to make patterns out of soaked reeds. The teacher then asked us to write a reflective essay about our privilege compared to people in the "real Nepal."

After I step off the motorbike, I give them a hundred rupees I had saved.

"We pile this into our donation pool," the man says. "Don't get disheartened, my friend. Nepal has a lot to offer our youth and you have a lot to give. And why do you want to pay taxes in an already-rich country? Jai Nepal!" He shakes my hand, and they drive away, waving.

As I trudge home, every step feels like the weight of a prisoner walking to a sentence. Father calls. I ignore it. There is an option to reapply for the visa twice more, paying a hundred fifty dollars each time, but the chances get slimmer with every reapplication, and my reaction at the end probably killed any hope. With time, I might be able to accept this reality and even feel relieved from the pressure of America. I always wanted to go there—who doesn't want to go to America—but there were times when it felt like reading a book that everyone tells you to read, that it's good and you must like it, and you try very hard to like it because you don't want to disappoint others. If my parents hadn't sent me to an American school, I don't think I would care that much for America. I love Angelou, sure, but I also love Usha Sherchan. I'm in a rock band, but I listen more to Nepali folk pop. But the last thing I want to do is let my parents down.

I hear Bhandari uncle's laughter from the alley. It's nauseating. At the entrance to our flat, his shoes are left by the front door. I unfold the sharp blade out of the nail cutter. Although I had not planned this, my hands move quickly. I carve out a gash across the Nike logo. I'm tempted to rip it apart like gutting a fish, but that might make him get a new pair. This, he would have to wear like a rash on his skin.

Mother, who is sewing patterns on a pillow cover, comes to the door as soon as I enter; Father is pretending to be in conversation with Bhandari uncle, hiding his anxiety with a dignified calm.

"How did it go?" Mother says, searching my eyes.

All kinds of thoughts are racing in my head.

"I got it," I say with a smile. "I'm so stunned I don't even know how to express it." The words tumble out uncontrollably.

Mother looks at my face. "You don't *look* happy, son."

"I'm too overwhelmed, Ama. Really, I don't know what to do. I'm so, just so . . ."

"It may be days before it finally sinks in," Father says. His taut wrinkles loosen to form their own little smiles. He takes off his glasses and wipes his eyes with his sleeves.

Granny mumbles something inaudible.

In an alcove behind the kitchen, where idols of Shiva, Ganesha, and Parvati are neatly arranged on the counter, Mother rings out the prayer bell.

"How does the visa look, son? Let me see?" Father says.

"I'll get it tomorrow. They've asked me to collect it tomorrow. That's the rule."

"Yes, that is their policy," Bhandari uncle says, avoiding eye contact with me.

Father murmurs something, and feeling for some loose change in his pockets, he walks out the door but comes back immediately, asking me if I am absolutely sure that I got it.

The fragrance of incense smoke wafts from the kitchen.

"Of course, Baba," I say. "Long interview. I'll tell you everything later."

He asks me to rest and walks out. I go to my room, close the door. My legs, unable to bear the burden, start trembling. I slump to my bed, breathing heavily.

In the next fifteen minutes or so, Baba brings a group of neighbors, men and women, whose chatter and laughter fill up the house.

"I always thought of him like my own son," Bhandari uncle says.

"Friends, we would like to invite you back tomorrow for a celebration as soon as the visa is brought home. We would like to see it first," Baba says. "Better to be absolutely certain. You never know with these things."

"Ever the pessimist," Bhandari uncle says. People laugh. I hear ice clinking in glasses and whiskey being poured. I know Baba had kept a bottle of Johnny Walker behind a pile of clothes in his cupboard. I crack open the door and peep out.

"Take a drink," Father says to Ama, who gulps down a neat shot of whiskey. I have seen her drink occasionally, but never after offering a prayer. Everyone cheers. Someone turns on the music on their phone and links it up to a portable speaker. The power goes out. Baba switches on the emergency light. It too flickers, creating a nightclub vibe with its short bursts of strobes. Ama breaks into an impromptu dance, moving her left hand in a circle, toes inches off the ground, up and down, up and down, mimicking the treadle of a sewing machine. These adults, in desperate need of a celebration, enjoy a momentary plunge into carelessness.

"Where is the man of the moment?" someone asks.

I shut the door.

"He's taking a rest," Father says.

"Call him, call him," Bhandari uncle says.

There is a loud knock. Baba stands in front, beaming with a smile, which quickly fades when he sees the shock on my face.

"Sanjay, Sanjay." Granny's voice is almost drowned out in the noise of revelry. More people stream in, laughing, calling each other out. People want to shake my hand. I sit next to Granny, who places her hand on my head.

"How was school?" she says. "Children must play. Go and play."

She squints. "How old are you now?" she asks.

"Nineteen."

"I had your father at that age. Then six more tumbled out, one by one, every year. This hole turned into a tunnel. You could ram a bus into it." She points to her crotch, smiling without teeth.

I smile too, feeling a faint sense of release. In a way, we both are nearing the end of our chapters, awaiting the results in anticipation. I rub her hand, lulling her to sleep.

~

Sometime in the course of the evening, my mother finds me sitting by myself.

"Is everything okay, Sanjay?" she asks. Something about her soft voice breaks me.

"I didn't get it. I lied. I didn't get the visa," I say choking back a sob.

The music stops. I feel like a thief robbing them of their joy. A brittle silence hangs over.

"Perfect timing," someone quips.

They leave one by one, some smirking. Others comfort my parents.

My father looks like he might collapse.

"Are you sure?" he asks. The evening sun, through the window, dapples on the floor creating a weird mismatch with the strobe lights.

Only Mother looks me calmly in the eye. "We'll be fine, don't worry," she says. "We have two more chances to apply. If we still don't get, we'll think about the next step." She uses the word "we" deliberately, then adds, "What hurt was your lie, Sanjay."

"I don't want to go back there. Not anytime soon. If that is how they humiliate us in the embassy, imagine the humiliation in their country."

"Don't be silly. There are thousands of Nepalis living there with dignity," Baba says. "The visa interview is calculated to filter out bad apples. You are not one of them."

I don't cry. Somehow tears seem inadequate to express my grief.

"Remember that time when I wanted to join the local theater group, and you insisted I take a piano lesson, and we argued, and at the end, none of us got what we wanted because I refused to learn piano? I was tired of doing things for you," I say to Ama.

"What is your point?" she asks.

"I need some time to think about this. What about what I want?"

"So, all this time, you did this for us? Is that what you're saying? Son, you wanted a Statue of Liberty for your thirteenth birthday. Not just any statue but one that glows in the dark. You put it next to your bed," Baba says.

"Because this is important for you—this, this dream of the American life. All I want is for you to be proud of me."

"You're hurt," he says. "Your words are bruised. They're not making sense."

"You have to learn to grab your chances, Sanjay," Ama says. "Your father never learned to do that. I learned that very late."

"Why is this about me, now?" Baba says.

Bhandari uncle must have been standing at the door for a while. "Who did this?" he asks, holding up the shoe.

Baba has a bewildered look. "It must be the street kids. That's why we don't leave expensive shoes by the door," he says. Bhandari uncle probably suspects the truth, but he doesn't want to confront Baba and lose a pliant friend.

"Please leave us alone in this moment, dai," Mother says, and he turns away with a scowl on his face.

I tell them about the interview, step by step. They seem to take solace in the fact that the business card had messed it up. I also tell them about the part where I accused the interviewer of bias. I could have left that out to end the day on a note of hope, but what good would come from setting up false hope?

"We'll try again," Father says. He and Mother sit beside me on Granny's bed. I rest my head on Mother's shoulder. She holds Baba's hands, and we fall into an embrace. Granny mumbles a prayer, oblivious of the day's events.

"Did you do that to Bhandari uncle's shoes?" Mother asks.

My silence confirms their suspicion. Even if they find it amusing, they don't laugh.

"That is not who we are," Father finally says.

"I know, Baba. I'm sorry."

I will apply again. I need to give it another shot after how far I've come. My parents will scrounge up enough cash. If we fail, we will at least have the memory of the party when Mother drank whiskey and danced in reckless joy. That brief moment will haunt us while she rattles the sewing machine, foraging for a new dream, long into the night.

The Diversity Committee

"Our next hire must be a person of color," Tanisha says. The only Black professor in this small, liberal arts college in Caldwell, Idaho, she is a postcolonial scholar, known to vanquish arguments by dispatching Spivak with piquant efficacy.

"There are more pressing issues than optics," Tim says. "The economy is a shitstorm. Our first-gen students are struggling to stay in college without financial support. We can't just talk about racial injustice."

"Race and class are inextricable," Tanisha says.

"Not in Idaho," Tim says.

"So, you're saying White is not a race?"

"What do we want to prioritize?" he asks.

When Tanisha and I were hired the same year in English, it was seen as a sort of a coup, but not every department is in a rush to hire Brown and Black professors. Tanisha and I have our differences, though; the biggest one is that she's an African American from Atlanta. I'm from Nepal, on a work visa. I live in fear of losing my visa if I don't toe an invisible line, or if I fail to publish a book soon. I'm good at finding creative ways to feel insecure, generally in life, but in a Trumpian America, the fear of getting deported is a lonely, single-minded fear. A colleague from Egypt had pulled me aside at the cafeteria and said, "Better to stay out of controversies." I wanted to challenge him. I was hired to be a

new voice, not a meek foreigner tormented by the trappings of paper-
work. But every day in this college is a test of finding that sweet spot
between being different and not too different.

~

"Want to get coffee?" Tanisha says after we leave the meeting.

The air has the crispness of early fall, and we pick a table in the
quad.

"How did Tim even get on the diversity committee?" I say.

"This whole thing is a charade. I feel like I took the wrong train to a
strange country," Tanisha says.

We chat about our classes and when the bells in the clock tower
building chime, I get up to leave.

"Let's grab Indian soon," she says. "How about that butter chicken
recipe you've been promising?"

"You mean chicken sandeko—it's a Nepali salad. We don't do butter
chicken."

"I did not know that," she says, wide-eyed.

~

It's a strange dynamic, ours. Tanisha is not only a compatriot, so to
speak, but my only competition. In this small college where classes
are frequently canceled due to low enrollment, our courses on minority lit often clash for attention; yet we are bound by a deeper anxiety of
being where we don't belong. We catch up once a month to chat, and
if it's Friday, a day uniquely poised to infiltrate our imagination with
complacency, coffee might extend into cocktails at a downtown bar
where Tanisha's partner, Jennifer, joins us. Tanisha has an intelligent
curiosity about India, its postcolonial economy, farmer protests, rise of
Hindutva. We argue about nuances, but when I remind her that Nepal
was never colonized and try to steer the conversation to Nepal-specific
issues, her interest fades. She had introduced me to Jennifer as a South
Asian, then seeming to realize my discomfort with that broad term,
had said, Nepalese, though I would have preferred the more accurate
Nepali.

"How's Literatures from the Himalayans?" she hollers as I'm heading to class.

"Not a single student of color. I'm glad Paige signed up, though."

"Keep her in your corner," Tanisha says.

The only reason Literatures from the Himalayans survived cancellation is because it fulfills the "global consciousness" requirement, meaning a bunch of bored students sign up to check off a box on their transcript. Not Paige. Her blue hair shines like glorious chrome against her tattooed white skin, and her copy of Manjushree Thapa's *The Tutor of History* is bursting with colorful notes.

"The US hegemony has something to do with Nepal's political upheavals," she says.

"What does America have to do with an obscure third-world country?" Caleb asks.

"If America hadn't listed Maoists as a terrorist organization, maybe, just maybe, their insurgency would have been legitimized in the world's eye," Paige says. "And can we please stop saying third world? It's racist."

"So, we can't even say third world anymore?" Caleb asks. His buddies smirk. They sit at the back of the classroom, teetering on the edge of adulthood with their skateboards and Vans sneakers.

"Why don't you do some research and share it with us next week, Caleb?" I ask. "I'll put you on the schedule." I say it with a Nepali accent, like *shedule*. Caleb smiles.

"I meant schedule."

Now, Paige looks at me and shakes her head.

After class, she comes to my office and apologizes.

"We're so responsible for fucking up the world," Paige says.

"We?"

"White people."

"What about all the great contribution to civilization by 'the Whites?'" I say, using air quotes.

"Yeah, right," she says, rolling her eyes, even though I was only half joking.

I tell her she's the last person that needs to apologize. She tells me about a research paper she's cowriting with Tanisha about the impact of colonialism on the Kenyan safari industry.

"The legacy of White colonialism is more nuanced than straight up rape and pillage," I say as we walk to the parking lot.

Paige spits out a little laugh. "Shouldn't we confront the abuser first? At least acknowledge the violence so assholes like Caleb learn to respect the struggles of colonized people?"

"Caleb is not scared of his ignorance. That's the problem. It's called apathy. Maybe it's a phase. Maybe he'll grow out of it. I've seen students change in four years."

"You're too nice," she says.

"What would *you* do if you were in my place?" I ask.

"Challenge him when he says that White people have saved the world?"

"He didn't say that."

"Well, when you add up everything he says, it's pretty fucking clear that he believes in White supremacy. Tanisha does a really good job of landing a hard blow when she needs to. There isn't a soft word for rape."

Paige has a smile on her face, a finely calibrated note of disapproval. I have always felt a desperate need for her to like me. When she extends her arms, I find myself moving in for a hug. I hug her tightly, her breasts pressed firmly against my chest, as my hand gently rubs her back. I feel her body get tense and I let go of the grip.

"Bye now," she says without making eye contact. She looks confused as she walks to her car.

As soon as I'm in my car, I send her a text. *I'm so sorry. I didn't mean it to be awkward.* Feeling the need to reassure her further, but not knowing how, I debate if I should just call, but I don't.

∿

At night, while I'm grading overdue assignments at home, a fear burrows and expands inside me like a tumor. I wonder if I should send Paige an email since she hasn't responded to my text. I don't want to confront the possibility that I might have had the wrong intention. I didn't. It really was meant to be an innocuous hug, but I'm also fully aware that it's not about the intention but the impact. I teach that stuff all the time, and I wince at the possibility that I might be capable of turning into a David Lurie kind of a wretched stereotype. When the Harvey Weinstein scandal broke out, I had taught Coetzee's *Disgrace*, thinking it might spark an interesting discussion in the wake of the #MeToo movement, totally unprepared for the disgust that the students felt toward David Lurie, a fifty-something professor who sleeps with his student and ponies up her grades. I had tried to reason that the novel's portrayal of Lurie was nuanced and we were underreading him by reducing him to a good vs. evil binary. The students were having none of it. They questioned my choice of the novel. Paige's response, though, had been more astute: "The rape is a violent performance committed by a man drunk on a toxic mix of patriarchy and White supremacy. While holding Lurie accountable, let's not ignore the system that enables his crime."

In the printed-out copy that I handed back to her in class, I had given it an A+ with a highly complimentary note and a smiley face next to my signature. She had looked right back at me with a smile and a discreet thumbs-up.

As the night wears on, I get more anxious about whether I'm overreacting. I can't talk to Tanisha about this. What would I even tell her? I call Saagar, a buddy from Nepal, who's in a residency program at UCLA, soon to become a cardiac surgeon.

Before coming to the United States on a student visa for graduate school, I had been an indifferent college student in Kathmandu who spent his weekends drinking beer in a dark Thamel bar, ogling at female budget travelers. Seeing European women mingle with Nepali tourist guides, drinking cheap beer in their dyed bohemian trousers, navels carelessly exposed, made the world seem smaller, distances between spaces shrunk. Nepali girls, even the most modern, could be privately prudish. There was a tacit acceptance, though I never knew from firsthand experience, that Nepali women would wear short skirts, even drink and smoke in bars, but would fend off any sexual moves because there was a line of modesty they didn't cross before marriage. These White women, on the other hand, came to Nepal to be anonymous and free. They knew the secret places of the world known only to adventurers but looking at them from a corner, they were also vulnerable to human oddities like arguing with each other in their own language, perhaps about money or relationships. They seemed like people destined to succeed but fumbled and failed along the way, and though we'd occasionally muster the courage to say, "Hi, where are you from?" mostly we admired them from afar. Saagar had been a core member of our group. We called ourselves the Dry Martinis.

~

I catch him in his off-hours. "You sound guilty," Saagar says.

"I shouldn't have rubbed her back. It's just that part I can't get out of my mind."

"Are you attracted to her?" he asks in his matter-of-fact doctor voice. "The age difference . . . what is it? Twelve, thirteen years? It's not that much."

"I mean attracted is such a complex word. Sure, she's beautiful. But I don't . . . I can't . . . think of her in that sense. She's my student. You know what it is? It's the deep-rooted fantasy of White women we can't shake off. Those damn feelings are stuck like maggots in our brains."

"Speak for yourself," he says. "I can't even look at a body anymore without thinking of atria and ventricles."

"The thing about this student. I mean, she's the best. Diligent, smart. And she really gets me."

"You want to fuck her," he says.

"Don't say that."

"I'm sure you'll be fine. You've always been an overthinker. You were also the most desperate dog in our group. You haven't changed."

I don't tell Saagar that I regularly scroll through Paige's Instagram, at least a few times a week, which means I have seen every picture she has ever posted. But I have stopped short of going further in my imagination.

I block her out of my mind. I don't know if it's the fear that it might break my soul if I took that leap.

Paige shows up in the next Literatures from the Himalayans class two days later. She's not her ebullient self, sits somewhere in the middle, sort of avoids eye contact, though she looks at me in a normal way when she participates in the discussion. There's no obvious sign of diffidence and I don't go out of my way to single her out or talk to her after class. I've given this a long, hard thought. I'm just as fallible as the next person, but I'll try harder to be a better human and a professor. In due time, if she's comfortable, I will redeem myself by possibly sponsoring Paige's internship, or guide her through some grant-based research. I won't go anywhere near her Insta, will not give her essay undue attention, will smile normally if I run into her, and generally stay out of her way unless she seeks me out. In the last two days, I've felt like a live chicken who knows the hatchet is coming down on him. It's not just the fear of repercussion but my own moral dilemma that I've never fully reflected on. I'm not even interested in the truth because of how clichéd the premise is: older male professor is attracted to a younger female student. But doesn't it happen to everyone? Isn't it human quirkiness to be tempted by transgression, to lean on tender moments of love that life throws at you from unexpected quarters? They're meant to be transient, these feelings, not dwelled upon and acted on, and in the privacy of one's own mind, morality is just a word. If it fulfills an emotional need, it can't be that bad, and yet, every time I go on her Instagram, the guilt sits like a low, unceasing bubble in the depth of my heart. I've replayed the hugging incident so much in my mind, I've struggled to sleep, and I'm somewhat relieved to see no real resistance from Paige.

When I swing by Tanisha's office after class, my plan is to hang around by her door just enough to gauge her reaction, but she asks if I have some time and closes the door behind me.

I'm nervous, but she talks about a research paper she's writing with Paige and asks for reading recommendations about coloniality and tourism in South Asia. We trade notes then the topic veers to Tim. Tanisha wants to run for chair next semester in the diversity committee and so does he. There will be an internal vote among the seven committee members, and Tanisha needs my support. Truth is, I've had an eye on the position as well. Early this year, I was upset when Tanisha got the diversity summer grant that we both had applied for. I was relying on the grant to fund my research trip to Nepal. When the announcement came, it felt like a kick in the ribs after finding out that she had convinced the dean that her work on race was more urgent. I make a mental note that this might not be the best time to gaze off into my soul, though I do feel like I'm being shafted by her.

"You have my vote," I say.

She gives me a hug with a gentle pat as I'm on my way out. "I appreciate you. Let me know if I can help in any way," she says.

~

This momentary sense of relief doesn't last. Paige's email shows up in my inbox later that day. It's a link to the college's Title IX page. I open the link with trepidation, and I'm directed to the definition of sexual harassment: "Unwelcome verbal, physical, or visual sexual conduct . . . harassment of a sexual nature that interferes with an individual's right to an education and participation in a program or activity." There is a separate link to a video made by the college's Title IX coordinator in which she explains the various forms of sexual harassment. I've watched this video during an online mandatory training program, where I had paid scant attention to most of the content, thinking it would never apply to me. The email doesn't have any other remark, nor is there is a salutation or sign-off. Bereft of any communication to give it cushion, the links appear cold against a vast white space.

"Hi, Paige, hope all is well. Can I ask what this is about?" I type before deleting it. I decide not sending a response would be prudent. I don't know how many times I check the email to see if she has written anything else, tossing and turning all night, barely getting any sleep.

~

Saagar's text the next day says that I'm overreacting: *It was just a hug, chill.* But I think my fear is palpable to Paige, and therefore she is overthinking it too, but maybe she has self-doubts as well, hence the surreptitious email without any assertive comments. It was just a hug, a weird, uncomfortable hug.

~

The architecture of the campus is Georgian with red-brick buildings. Footsteps echo in the hallways.

"Rakesh, thanks for coming," Dean Melissa May says. She has called for this meeting to discuss my upcoming contract renewal and I'm not sure if this has anything to do with what has transpired with Paige, or a possible Title IX investigation. A strand of pearls matches May's dark business suit, not the usual attire for this recent biology professor turned dean. The room smells of coffee. I politely decline a paper cup that she pours from a stainless carafe.

She says this is a routine meeting and goes over the contract review process, and I see no sign that she has caught on to something. Even if she did, she wouldn't get involved in a Title IX investigation unless called in as a witness. I knew that much about how investigations worked. Before I leave, she says there's one more thing. She closes the door.

"There's a rumor about you," she says, "that you make some female students uncomfortable by the way you look at them."

"Sorry?"

"It's been dropped into my ears by some students. Apparently, it's an open secret. They've said—how should I put it—that you stare."

I can't believe what I'm hearing.

"Who are the 'they' you're referring to?" I ask.

"I had two students from one of your classes drop into my office. This was about a week ago. I didn't want to alarm you but thought you should be made aware."

I shrug, slightly relieved that it couldn't be Paige if this happened a week ago.

"Do you think it might be cultural?" she asks.

"What do you mean?" I know exactly what she means, and she's, of course, partially right, but I don't want to grant her that.

"Maybe some communication miscues that could be ironed out?"

"I'm hearing this for the first time." My voice almost cracks.

"Let me know if I can help you navigate through this," she says. She suggests a few training programs. "We all have our blind spots. Most of it is unintentional. I don't mean to cause any distress, and it certainly hasn't been reported as a formal complaint. Just something to think about."

I sit in silence, keeping within myself whatever it is I'm feeling, which is a whole lot of embarrassment.

"That may mess with my visa," I say, as if that should be on top of everyone's mind.

"Why would it?" she says.

This person whom I have once sat next to in a faculty meeting, small-talking our way through grading nightmares and disproportionate work-pay load, is now trying to mask a mixture of pity and repulsion in her eyes.

~

"Didn't you have a Spanish girlfriend once?" Saagar asks. I'm making dinner and have him on speakerphone.

"I think about her a lot," I say.

Clara was my first-ever girlfriend. We met in North Carolina, where I was in a master's program and she was an undergraduate exchange student, majoring in theater. We lived in the same international dorm and would wait for each other to have dinner in the cafeteria, some-times eating off a single plate. We loved reading the same books and discussing them afterward. That's how I read *Angels in America*. She read the first half and I the second. Our first sex was on a flagstone path in Coker Arboretum at midnight, partially hidden behind a shrub of perennials. She was wearing a skirt with nothing underneath, and we could hear some boys playing frisbee in the distance as we locked into hungry, sweaty sex. We discovered a love for baked tilapia with a dash of lime when we moved into an apartment; we worked hard in our classes, went on hikes along the Bolin Creek trail, and made love every-where and anywhere, including standing, with her back against a tree. My need for her was insatiable. She said that when we made love, I looked at her so intensely that she felt as though I had thrust my hand into her chest. After a year, she moved back to Barcelona and that was it. We never really contacted each other again.

"Remember when you went after that Israeli woman in Thamel?" Saagar asks.

"I didn't go after her, don't exaggerate."

"You were drunk and tried to butt your way between her and this other guy she was dancing with. We had to drag you away and get the hell out before we were pummeled by the local guys."

"Embarrassing," I say.

"You were always so fucking desperate," he says. "You're still like that. You're a weirdo, man. Reading your crazy books and living alone in rural Idaho."

"Weren't we all like that? I mean, we were in a culture where that wasn't seen as a problem. Actually, I shouldn't say culture. It's funny how I fall into these traps of stereotypes, even though I'm constantly telling my students not to generalize. Of course, not every man in Nepal thinks like that, but you know what I mean? Our circle. It wasn't that removed from a typical male mentality in Kathmandu."

"You were always a bit more savage. The way you talked about those women."

I'm not shocked at his pathetic attempts to put me down. It makes the man feel better about himself, and I let him have it.

"I wasn't. Come on, that's harsh," I say.

"Some of us had girlfriends, remember?" he says.

"*You* did and eventually moved out of our group."

"It was so feral, and you still sound like that."

"Stop it, man," I say. "What's next? You'll soon earn a six-figure salary. You have an eye on a BMW 5 Series. You're engaged to your beautiful Nepali girlfriend. I need to get out of Idaho . . . get out of a job that pays peanuts. Grow up, Saagar," I say and hang up.

We talk once every few months and always end up this way, him gloating about houses and cars, or putting me down one way or another, and me promising not to talk to him again. I try to forget about it, pour myself a fourth glass of IPA, and throw chopped zucchini and onions into a lentil batter. The smell of cumin and the sizzle of oil provide a momentary relief from the stress. After Clara, I didn't feel a need to get into another relationship. Didn't really feel the need for sex, either. When I did, there were strip clubs and the occasional escort. I just fell into my books and a PhD program. Thinking of Clara now, I lie on the couch and watch a YouTuber's vlog about Barcelona. I don't feel like getting up to eat. It requires an act of courage that I don't have.

Later Saagar sends a text: *I wasn't trying to be harsh. You ARE a damn loner, but you're taking this way too seriously. You'll be fine, and that student chick is probably into you, anyway.*

I don't respond. In any case, I need a break from him, and his casual misogyny disguised as banter.

At least I'm not sexist, at least not in a conscious way. I try to better myself, I write back and add a smiley face with a wink.

Yawn, good luck, he writes back.

~

The next few weeks, I'm intent on being a competent professor, adequately affable. Paige shows up to every class, always in jeans, deviating so obviously from the shorter skirts. I try to curb my habit to turn to her for a response. She hasn't completely retreated into a shell, I think, and participates sufficiently, though she has taken to doodling. How do people find a sense of proportion by drawing chaotic shapes in their notebook? Of course, I avoid looking at her, but she and I both know that my mental gaze penetrates her so thoroughly that she is sensitive every time she shifts her posture in the chair. And how is it that I notice when she scratches her leg, even when my desire is to be inconspicuous behind a computer cabinet? Is my peripheral vision deliberately lustful and I never realized it? Standing behind the cabinet, I have become acutely aware of the stains on the carpet, the disorganized posters trapped behind a mesh of ugly Scotch tape. One poster, advertising a campus event, is so disturbingly yellow, I'm surprised I'd never noticed it, which must be an indication of my dedication to the content of the course.

I have also been reading reviews on Rate My Professor. Fortunately, the bad comments are rare, but they are noticeable. Someone wrote that

I stare at her and make her uncomfortable. Another person responded that it may be cultural. It's apparently normal to "stare" in some cultures, someone else has written. Do I really stare, or maybe my eyes naturally brush against parts of their bodies I'm not supposed to look at, and what does it say about my character that I have been so utterly unaware of my own gestures, my motivations? I feel so brittle standing before them now that as soon as I walk into the classroom, I go behind a beige cabinet stacked with drawers and an ugly desktop computer. At least it hides half my body. My affable personality has cracked. I give them long stretches of solo or group assignments, and the silence is so thick, Caleb's sneers and yawns have become bolder.

In the hallways, I walk with my head down because I can't trust my eyes anymore. Everyone seems to be whispering behind my back. Maybe they always did, and I never noticed. The senseless confidence of their smiles has disappeared; they avoid bumping into me. Am I overthinking all this or is word actually getting around? I have avoided Tanisha since I saw her last. I won't be able to cope with her oblivious niceness, or the devastating disappointment in her eyes. With most colleagues, there is a relaxing sense of apathy that makes it easy to get in and out of conversations. Tanisha, on the other hand, holds on to a tantalizing shimmering quality that she sees in me, an affirmation that her intellectual pursuits, her very existence, is not futile in this isolated place, that there is at least me, and a few others like me, who lean on each other for some greater good of advancing the legitimacy of minority groups. If she found out that I have sexual fantasies about a student, I would be a betrayal to the whole cause.

Then the janitor comes into my office in a cowboy hat. I have started wearing dark glasses when I'm not in a classroom, and he looks at me in a peculiar way. He wants to empty out my wastebasket. I find the hat intrusive. Where is the usual Mexican fellow who comes to collect trash? Is this White man checking in on me?

In my high school in Nepal, the American ambassador had once been a guest of honor at a musical event, a day that turned into an unintentionally funny experience. It was Nag Panchami, a festival devoted to snakes, so our geriatric principal, quivering under the shadow of the ambassador's cowboy hat, invited a snake charmer to entertain the guest. Without being prompted, the ambassador picked up the cobra and held it, unperturbed by the reptile's bobbing head and flickering tongue. The whole auditorium clapped, dazzled by the man's prowess. When he tipped his hat to the audience, it felt like he was acknowledging an authority pliantly handed to him.

"The garbage can, sir," the man says. I've never seen him before.

"Could you not wear that cowboy hat in my room, please? I mean, it's a symbol of a particular brand of White American masculinity and exclusion."

He stands, unsure of what to do. "You have an accent. Where you from?" That's the only comeback he can think of. Before I can respond, he shakes his head and leaves.

At night, I open the link to the Title IX video. It shows animated characters victimized by stalkers and harassers in seemingly normal situations. One video shows a female student's book dropping accidentally from her backpack in the library. An older man, possibly a professor, picks it up and follows her all the way to the parking lot instead of giving the book to her immediately. His whole vibe is that of a stalker, violating her privacy, and the cartoon treatment of the video accompanied by elevator music gives it an eerie effect. After the animation, the college's Title IX coordinator talks about the blurred line between consent and assault. I stare at the screen, feeling like a dark reality is pressing down on me. I'm relieved to get a text from Tanisha: *See you at the meeting tomorrow.* I had totally forgotten about the diversity committee meeting. The time has come to throw our hats in the ring for the chair position. Also, she actually sent me a text. I read it several times. There isn't the usual banter like, hey stranger. At the same time, she did write to me in six simple words without any sign of distress. *We'll make it the BIPOC inquisition*, I reply with a smiley face.

It's a late-afternoon meeting. I put my sunglasses in my pocket as I show up a few minutes late. Tanisha gives me a nod. The rest are looking at their laptops. The next forty minutes are spent discussing the addition of a diversity statement in the faculty manual. Some of us argue that when a faculty member is up for promotion, they should include a statement in their portfolio that mentions their contribution to diversity, equity, and inclusion. Tim disagrees because not everyone, apparently, has a background in diversity. As usual, Tanisha is the most vocal advocate. I chime in once or twice. Tim is uncharacteristically subdued, preoccupied as he seems with the impending vote. A decision on the manual is postponed and it's time to cast our ballots. My name is up there on a website with all seven members. I toy with a temptation to vote for Tim just to fuck things up. If I vote for myself, Tanisha will see that as a betrayal, even though the votes are anonymous—but who else would vote for the reticent Rakesh? May would probably rule it out, anyway, after her comment about the rumors. It's clearly a battle between Tim and Tanisha. Everyone knows that. I move the cursor on my laptop between her name and mine, then hers and Tim's. There is nothing sinister in my intent. I only think of this as momentarily funny. I click on Tanisha. She wins by four to three votes.

Walking to the parking lot together, Tanisha is genuinely excited. She talks about everything that can be done to make a difference through the diversity committee. She also seems excited to collaborate with me and I'm relieved to know that she hasn't heard anything. She asks me how I am, comments on my stubble, goes on a rant about one of her classes, talks briefly about her research, drops a line about Jennifer's apparent tardiness, then asks me about me, not disappointed by my rather terse response, and picks up where I leave off about a perfunctory teaching remark. She's like a saxophone player in an orchestra, solid as a brick but nimble to blend and listen, before returning out front for a remarkable solo. She mostly seems happy to see me, and I'm so relieved at the ease between us, I put my arm around her.

"I appreciate you," I say, giving her a side hug, and I mean that. She has been a steady friend—the intervention of pure reason.

"I fucked up," I tell her, and it all comes pouring out. I tell her about the hug and Paige's email with the Title IX links. We have stopped walking, and she is listening with a hand covering her cheek. My impulsive candor turns quickly into anger. Against myself. I can't believe I just cracked. There is no anger or urgency in Tanisha's face, at least not visibly. I feel a taste of acid in my mouth that I swallow because I decide that she would be offended if I spat it out. Even though I feel like my mind is racing and I'm talking too much, I actually keep it short, emphasizing that the text message was what tipped it over—that was a mistake, because the hug itself was harmless. I try to walk a fine line to make myself neither the victim nor the offender.

"I didn't do it on purpose, because I had no intention of causing all this," I say, which is the truth.

She doesn't speak for a while, just keeps looking at the ground with her hand still on her cheek. Finally, she says, "Are you okay? How have you been holding up?"

"I'm fine. I really am. I'm more concerned about Paige."

We continue walking and she says, "We had a long chat yesterday about our research project. She's still doing all her work. She's excellent that way, but she has seemed a bit distant. She said she feels guilty about things, but she didn't say what. I thought it had something do with her family. There are some unresolved issues there." As soon as she says this, I see a flash of anger travel fast to her eyes. In a moment of frailty, she also cracked and spoke too much. She tries to take it back and says that maybe guilt wasn't exactly the word Paige used, maybe it was, "bad . . . she felt bad, which, I guess, is only natural."

I am too scared to extract any more information. I dread to think that Paige is feeling guilty. She shouldn't, and I don't feel any perverse lucidity in realizing that the blame has somehow shifted from me. Strangely, though, hearing that, I also feel like I can make amends. Maybe time will be the healer. I will exist in a safe distance from her, and when the time is right, I will apologize and help untangle, if I may, the possible knots of confusion and anger. More than I have ever felt, I resolve to regard Paige as an excellent student who I will help learn and grow.

"Now, do I have to report this as an alleged Title IX since we're mandatory reporters?" Tanisha asks.

"No, but this isn't Title IX. Paige hasn't reported it." I'm not confident about this and wonder if I shot myself in the foot.

Tanisha sips water from her bottle. We walk quietly for a while, then she says, "I appreciate you sharing it with me. I'm sure things will eventually be fine. Let me know if you need to talk more or how I can help." She makes a point to look me in the eye when she says this, but she doesn't smile. The joy that she had felt prior to my revelation seems to have snapped from her heart.

When we reach my car, Tanisha says, "Eeww." In the car next to mine, stuck behind the wiper, is a note with the word *Creep!* We immediately know that it was meant for me but play along with her amusement.

"What's *that* all about?" she says with a quick laugh.

I sigh. Then I shrug. And sigh again.

"Are you okay?" she asks.

"I need a fucking drink. It's been a long week."

"You take care, okay?" she says. She waves absentmindedly.

On the one hand, I feel relieved; on the other hand, I'm distressed. My guilt is curable if I do not repeat the mistake, that is, if I don't make my feelings about any student apparent. It is called being professional. Maybe I do have an uncurable lustful eye, and that is okay if I keep it in check. Between the feeling and the act, a whole ocean lies. I'll go to therapy. I'll be a better human and a teacher, for Paige and other Paiges of my world. I'm still standing when Tanisha glances back at me. Her eyes dart to the car next to mine. She sees that the note is no longer there. It's scrunched in my palm. She keeps walking. We unlock our cars; the sounds of our keys reverberate in this near-empty lot. I plop down in the seat.

There isn't an exact word for creep in Nepali. The closest word, boka, courses through me. Boka is a horny male. Someone who stares. "Calm down, everything will be just fine," I tell myself as I watch her drive slowly out of the parking lot.

Dry Blood

Ma surreptitiously walked into her daughter's room. Meena's phone lay on her bed. Ma picked it up, typed the password, and quickly scrolled through Meena's text messages. Meena had lately been spending hours in her bedroom with an older man under the pretense of writing a script for a play, and Ma was desperate to find out what was going on because a girl in Nepal, regardless of wealth, could end up paying an enormous price for misusing her freedom.

Ma's anxiety about her daughter's future had grown steadily over the past few months. Meena's older brother was a law student at Harvard, and Meena was expected to follow the family tradition, but since graduating from high school with distinction, the girl had taken up a strange obsession with poetry, drama, and men—in what order was anyone's guess. Ma looked at a string of chats Meena had been having with that man, Deepak, but couldn't find anything scandalous, just things about books, though the heart emojis seemed wholly unnecessary.

"She'll be out of the shower any minute," the maid said, standing at the door in Meena's bedroom.

"Geeta, you scared me," Ma said. She put the phone back in her daughter's purse.

Later, Geeta brought a glass of water on a tray to the veranda, where Ma sat in an armchair under an awning covered with pink bougainvillea. The morning heat was intense. Streams of sweat trickled behind Ma's ears. It was Geeta who had leaked the password to Ma. In one of her generous moods, Meena had taught the maid how to watch You-Tube on her phone, but Ma knew where the maid's loyalty lay.

Geeta gently scraped out an aspirin from its wrapper and let it drop into the water, causing the liquid to sizzle. Ma took a sip, then rested her head in the groove of the chair as Geeta massaged her temples.

"How long has he been here?" Ma asked, referring to the man currently in Meena's bedroom. Apparently, he was a thespian, and a popular one at that. Ma couldn't stand the sight of him, his ponytail, his shabby kurta and jeans, and the unapologetic stench of cheap cigarettes that lingered around him. What would people say if they saw the daughter of Sunil Raj Joshi mingling with a thirty-something actor without a real job, right under Ma's nose? One nasty remark was enough to cut the man down to size, but Ma restrained herself, fearful of Meena's reaction.

The maid told her he was on his third cup of coffee.

"What do they do in there?" Ma said.

"Write scripts," Geeta said.

"Do you know how much trouble I went to in the market this morning? I'm tired of being treated like a slave in this house," Ma said.

"I'd go if you trusted me." For a twelve-year-old, Geeta had a sharp tongue, though she was right. Ma did all the grocery shopping and kept an account of every purchase. She recorded them in her diary under two columns: items and expenses.

With her thumbs, Geeta pressed the curve of Ma's eyebrows, rubbing away tiny morsels of pain.

"Can you believe those vendors fight like animals?" Ma said.

"Did you find anything on the phone?" Geeta asked.

"Mind your own business. I wouldn't tell you even if I did," Ma said, momentarily relieved that she hadn't, indeed, found anything indecent on her daughter's phone, though what exactly she was expecting to find, she didn't know.

The maid asked Ma if she needed another glass of water, but Ma was already scrolling down the screen on her own iPhone. She opened the stock market app and checked the latest index; her mind was elsewhere this morning. She knew that she struggled to tackle Meena's arrogance because she wasn't confident and cunning like her daughter. The night before her final exam Meena had come home past midnight, alcohol on her breath. Ma had fallen asleep on the sofa with her phone held to her chest. When she heard her daughter's scooter, she sat up and turned on the TV, pretending to watch a BBC documentary about Palestine. As Meena removed her shoes at the door, Ma watched her from the corner of her eyes. She knew Meena had drunk alcohol from the way she left a shoe upturned.

"Don't you know that's a bad omen?" Ma had said, but she got nothing but a shrug from Meena. Ma would've preferred an argument instead of this silent dismissiveness. Her daughter walked past her, and with alcohol-smelling breath said, "I went out with some friends. It's called a stressbuster. Besides, Dad doesn't have a problem." No further explanation was needed after this. Ma tipped the shoe over with her toe, irritated at Sunil, who could sleep through his daughter's midnight escapades.

~

"Geetu?" Ma called, using the nickname when she craved the maid's company.

The girl came running, wiping her wet hands with a mop tucked into the hem of her suruwal.

"Make me a cup of tea."

Geeta made tea and returned minutes later with the tea tray, which she placed on the side table. She put a spoon of sugar in the porcelain cup and stirred it carefully. Ma liked her tea piping hot, so the maid had to first heat the empty cup in a microwave and then pour the steaming tea into it. If it wasn't up to measure, she made Geeta throw it out and make a fresh cup all over again. Sometimes this process went on for a few rounds until Ma felt the temperature was just right to calm or complement her mood. It wasn't her intention to torture Geeta, but the chronic headaches she suffered from meant that she just had to be fussy about certain things.

"What are they up to?" Ma asked.

"The door is locked," Geeta said.

Ma gave her a look.

"They're writing a *play*," Geeta said. "It's about the plight of farmers."

"As if . . ."

"When I go in with coffee, I stand quietly and watch Meena dijju read, thinking how easily English flows from her mouth. She says she'll teach me to read like that. I guess there's still hope for a poor girl like me."

"Does he sleep on her bed?" Ma said.

"Hugging the pillow."

"Sit with me for a while. You can do the dishes later."

Geeta excused herself and returned with a bucket of soap-water and a dry piece of cloth tied around her wrist. She crouched down and started wiping the flowerpots placed along the trough of the veranda. How cheerful these flowers were—marigolds, geraniums, and roses. The geraniums were in full bloom at this time of the year. Ma had hand-picked the flowers from the nursery, running her fingers through the soil, often breaking apart clumps to check for moisture. It was her wish to grow her own garden in the vast compound behind the house where the voices of crows rang out from tall dark trees. Presently, the tea allowed Ma's thoughts to arrange themselves quietly.

She called Bishnu-ji, the family accountant, to query the latest report on the stock market. Nepal Lever's equity had shot up the day before and Ma sensed that it was trending upward.

"Let's wait until noon," the accountant said. "The protest announced by the opposition might disrupt the market. There's a rumor of street marches and disturbances."

"Call me when you find out more," Ma said and hung up. As always, the country was teetering toward collapse. Colleges were shut half the year due to this and that strike, and if Meena lost a year, she might be discouraged to apply to an Ivy League college the following year given her propensity to stray toward a world inspired by poverty. All Ma wanted was to give her daughter the opportunity for success that was denied to her all her life.

Geeta, meanwhile, watered the flowers, humming a jingle about girl education in shrill, high pitch, and a la Freddie Mercury—thanks to Meena's tutorial—she held the spout of the can like a microphone and in undecipherable English sang the words to "We Will Rock You." Ma tolerated all this nonsense because the girl was still a child, and truth be told, mildly entertaining, but what Ma hadn't expected was Geeta to run across the veranda mimicking the singer's stage moves, raising an arm with the water can, the other hand clenched in a fist. The word Queen had once dazzled Ma, right after marriage, when Sunil would constantly play from his vast vinyl collection, everything from Nepali folk to jazz and rock. Ma would run her finger along the spiral grooves, fearful and excited about some wonderful life waiting for her. She was jolted from her thoughts when the maid bumped into a Chinese vase that sat atop a glass table. The expensive vase toppled and shattered to pieces, each shard sparkling like ruby on the marble floor.

The crash left a lingering silence. Despite an inner voice telling her not to do it, Ma slapped the maid on the cheek. Geeta lost her footing and fell onto the broken glass, then quickly stood back up. A streak of blood trickled from her palm. Ma had reacted out of habit. "Forget it happened. No need to cry," she said. The girl's shoulders hunched like she'd been pressed down with the weight of shock, but she didn't cry.

"What was that sound?" said Meena, walking in through the screen door that partitioned the veranda. Her hair looked rumpled, and the man followed right behind. The mustard oil in his hair gave off a sharp odor.

Meena poked the maid's palm with her finger. "It's a deep cut. Go wash your hands. I'll put on a bandage," she said, and the maid left without making eye contact with Ma.

"It was an accident," Ma said.

"She needs a tetanus shot," the man said.

"Why are you after my daughter?" Ma asked him.

He didn't say anything. He simply rolled up the frayed sleeve of his kurta.

"Mom, stop," Meena said.

His feet were large and ugly, the dirt visible under his toenails. "What else do you do besides be a bad influence? Do you have a job?" Ma said.

"Meena volunteered to work with our troupe. We're writing a script," he said.

"I'll call you later," Meena said to him, touching him lightly on his arm. He stood defiantly, as if he wasn't prepared to give in to Ma's accusations.

"Do you know, madam, who I am?" he asked.

"I don't care who you are. You are an intruder in my house. How dare you invite yourself without my permission, sleep on my daughter's bed, drink my coffee all day? That tells me a lot about exactly the kind of person you are."

The man looked at Meena. "I'm glad you're not like them. Unchecked privilege. It's frankly shocking."

He said that and he left.

Meena followed him. They stood at the screen door for a moment. Meena whispered something to him. The man waved his palm indignantly and left.

"How dare you?" Meena said as she walked back to where Ma was.

"What about your college application?"

"What gives you the right to attack my friend?"

"Friend?"

"Did you hit Geeta?" Meena asked after a pause.

"What about your college application?"

"My SAT scores came in. 2200."

"That's wonderful. Why didn't you tell me?" Ma instinctively reached out her hand, but Meena flinched as one would at the touch of ice. "Are you using Geeta to spy on me now?" she asked.

"Does your dad know about your SAT score?"

"You think I'm having sex."

"I just want you to think about your future."

"You're so crazy," Meena said, slamming the screen door on her way out.

Forming the end of her sari into a knot, loosening and tightening it, Ma tried to console herself that the fault wasn't necessarily hers, but she regretted her action all the same. Her occasional slaps were discreet transactions between master and servant, meted out for minor lapses such as burnt toast. Geeta accepted that the slaps were simply Ma's way of marking her territory, a master's birthright, which the maid was not expected to complain about. They were especially not to be discussed with anyone else, least of all Sunil, who reacted very strongly against physical punishments. He never raised his hand to his daughter, and that one time when Ma had slapped Meena when the girl was eight years old, she had been held hostage to father-daughter silent treatment for days. Like a rash that she couldn't control, Ma instead slapped the maid occasionally. Nothing too harsh. A light slap here and there to keep the ducks in a row. Village girls were neither kids nor adults, uniquely equipped at inhabiting that indefinite space. Besides being momentarily stunned, Geeta would quietly move on, seemingly determined not to repeat her mistake, but a fresh headache now crept up Ma's temples. It became more and more obvious to her that she may have bequeathed her stubbornness to her daughter, a trait that for years Ma had carried like a bite mark on her body, examining it every morning and quietly nursing it all day, the consequence of Sunil's soft oppression.

Ma was barely nineteen when she married Sunil, who, at twenty-seven, had just returned from America with a law degree. Perhaps Sunil's parents—his father had been a judge in the supreme court and his mother one of the first trained nurses—felt that a government officer's daughter from a simple background inherently possessed the virtue of obedience, and on the suggestion of a commonly acquainted priest, their wedding was arranged. Ma quickly discovered that Sunil's opposition to her demure role in their marriage was a facade. He encouraged her to go to college, to pursue a career, but was irritated by her lack of knowledge about world affairs and implied that she'd be better off as a housewife. On her parents' insistence, Ma had dropped out of her BA degree to get married, and though she'd never been particularly fond of college, she felt like she'd made the bigger sacrifice. Ma had had no say in the marriage. She had been groomed to be respectful above all else. It was simply assumed that she would accept the offer, considering it had come from such a distinguished family. She met her future husband in her parents' tiny living room, surrounded by relatives from both sides who shared a murmured agreement about the auspicious union. With her head bowed down, Ma had lifted her eyes to look at Sunil, who sat opposite her. He had the eyes of a man devoted to books, and she instinctively felt that he would not have had too many encounters with women. As the wafts of aloo puri drifted through the open window, their marriage was confirmed, and the wedding date set in the same month.

Two weeks later Ma and Sunil were in New York City on their honeymoon. It was here that Ma realized that she did not really understand the world outside. The museums that Sunil insisted on visiting every day bored her. She would watch him from over the brim of her coffee cup as he gravely nodded at each sculpture, whose significance he would then try to explain to her while she smoothed the crease of her sari, not knowing what to say. At Strand, he bought her a copy of the *New Yorker*, a magazine that was so impossible to comprehend, it still aroused fearful pictures in her mind. In her halting English, she would try to read a few pages in their hotel room while Sunil hovered around expecting to see flashes of epiphany in her eyes. "Not even the cartoons?" he would ask. One time, Ma wept into the hotel towel in the bathroom, and perhaps sensing that she had cried, he stroked her hair and said, "Don't worry, you'll learn." He took her kayaking on the Hudson River, where they relied on each other to keep the skinny boat afloat. Their eyes locked as they stroked their paddles in a steady rhythm. "I love you," Sunil said for the first time, while Ma, too nervous that the weight of those words might tip the canoe over, devoted her entire concentration on paddling. When Sunil slept soundly in her arms at night, Ma felt secure in his embrace but knew that he had been quietly disappointed in her. Ma began to carry a silent resentment against an invisible fate for having so much power over her life. Their marriage had not been an inevitability, but a gamble. A visit to the New York Stock Exchange one day brought about some respite. Ma was fascinated with the electronic screens where numbers dazzled with the power to conjure up dread and hope, and those who gained were braced with a calculating instinct that a college degree could not provide. Seeing that she might finally be able to gamble on her own instincts, Ma asked Sunil about a career in stocks. He told her she shouldn't get into such fads.

Upon her return, however, Ma took to the lure of stocks. She nosed around the local stock market, visiting the office of the Nepal Stock

Exchange, where screens were replaced with white boards on which brokers wrote down numbers with a marker and erased them with their palms. Ma would stand in a corner observing how stocks were traded. She made a binder of cut-up newspaper articles and attempted to study market patterns, and she met Kiran-ji, a garrulous young broker. It may have been the sight of her Italian leather handbag, or her reticent posture in a room that reeked of male sweat that inspired Kiran-ji to give her unsolicited advice. Soon Ma was buying and selling shares with the brisk confidence of a professional. She acquired bonds, invested in assets, and made a small fortune that enabled her to open her own savings account from which occasional withdrawals were made for cherished expenses such as the mahogany door that she'd installed with her own money. What she failed to acquire was the respect of her husband, who viewed her interest in the stock market as a passable hobby. Sunil found it crude, this world of money and finance. It was not a noble occupation. He didn't mind that she controlled the finances at home, but despite his casual curiosity about Ma's incomes and investments, Sunil expected her to acquiesce to a degree of pliancy that enabled him to mold her into an ideal. He bought her gray-covered books on economics, which Ma didn't care for. He brought up the fact that his mother went to medical college after marriage, ending up as the head nurse in Bir Hospital. A professional career was not just about money, but an elevator to higher nobility, he said. But Ma was unwilling to make another big sacrifice for him. To salvage her self-pride, she even went to the extent of keeping Kiran-ji as a salaried employee, and yet, she pined for her husband's respect. "I've supported you, but we have little in common," he said and in her lone moments, Ma wondered if she had let her single-mindedness affect their marriage—if indeed a college education would have dignified her in her family's eyes. Her guilt for lack of trying gathered like a lump in her throat, and she was now preoccupied with the thought that her daughter too was showing signs of being a victim of her own ego, perhaps to graver consequences.

After the dull pounding of her temples dissipated, Ma picked up a broom and swept away the shards on the floor. If he found out, Sunil wouldn't stop fretting and lecturing about how domestic violence was now punishable by law in Nepal. The real violence was Sunil's apathy toward the maid. Geeta tiptoed on the periphery of his existence; their only one-on-one communication was limited to her serving his bedside tea every morning with the well-rehearsed "Thulo hajur, tea," which Sunil acknowledged with a "huncha ba" while his face remained buried under the quilt.

Hearing Sunil's car outside the gate, Ma tied her hair into a bun and straightened the crease of her sari. Her husband was on the phone as she entered the living room. When he saw her, he bunched his fingers toward his mouth signaling he was hungry, a routine gesture when he came home for lunch. Geeta hadn't had the time to prepare anything, and Ma couldn't ask Meena about the maid because Sunil would find out, so Ma allowed those concerns to drift away momentarily. From the fridge she took out the previous night's dal, chicken curry, and aloo kauli. Several minutes were spent finding the cilantro that Geeta had stuffed in the lowest compartment of the fridge as well as locating the methi seeds in the overhead cabinet. Ma fried the methi in a cauldron of hot oil, then poured the dal into it, making the lentil give off a *jhwaaaaiah* sound. In it went a handful of chopped cilantro for garnish, and another handful into the slow-burning chicken. Wistfully humming the Rajesh Khanna classic "Mere Sapano Ki Rani Kab Ayegi Tu," Ma wiped the glass plates with the kitchen towel. She could feel his presence then. Sunil stood behind her, running his fingertip along the curve of her neck.

"What are you doing?" she said with a giggle.

He hummed the song along with her and she felt the back of her neck grow warm from his breath.

"We should go on another honeymoon," he said.

Ma blushed. She turned around to face her husband.

"Where's the maid, by the way?" he said.

"Sick," she said. She played with the button of his shirt. Their eyes met. "You do appreciate how well I've managed this house, don't you?" she said.

"What's the matter today? Looks like the news about the strike has flustered you. I hear Nepal Lever's shares will drop like a dead bird."

"Daddy," Meena called from the living room.

Ma wrapped her arm around Sunil's waist.

"Dad, I need to talk to you about something."

Ma pulled him closer. "Don't leave me," she said.

"You're her mother. Act your age," he said.

This really hurt Ma. She released him from her grip instantly.

Meena appeared at the door. "Daddy, something urgent needs your attention," she said.

"I'm not a free man in this house," Sunil said aloud. He dismally looked at his wife. "Yes, darling," he said and followed his daughter.

Ma carried the dishes and set them on the dining table. Meena and her father had taken their rightful seats, already engrossed in a conversation about labor laws for which the strike was rumored to happen. Ma stood next to her husband and served him the chicken curry, pouring a ladleful over the steaming rice.

"How bad will this strike be?" she asked.

"Nothing on the news, yet," he said.

"The beet pickle has been drying in the sun all morning. You want me to get some for you?" Ma said.

"Not now," Sunil said.

Discussing Section 34 with her father, Meena went to the kitchen and brought her own plate, ignoring the one her mother had put in front of her.

"Not joining us?" Sunil turned around to ask his wife, who was now hovering behind his chair.

"I'm not hungry," she said.

He glanced at his daughter. "What happened to the maid, anyway?" he asked.

Meena cleared her throat.

"This maid seems reliable," he said.

"What about sending her to school, Daddy?" Meena said, fingering the rice and dal into a ball. "By the way, is this last night's food?"

"The maid is sick. Don't blame your mother," Sunil said.

"Anyway, don't dodge the topic, Daddy. Let's hear your argument."

"Let's get her admitted into a school. I have no problem. What does Ma think if the maid is gone the whole day? That's the real question," Sunil said.

Meena threw her arms in the air, a routine gesture at the dining table. "Such an elitist."

Swirling his finger in the dal bowl, Sunil looked at his daughter and said, "This is Ma's call."

Meena pointed her curry-stained finger at him: "That Churchill fellow said, 'The best argument against democracy is a five-minute conversation with the average voter.' You, your honor, are essentially the same breed," she said.

Father and daughter's eyes were now locked. Soon Meena would wave her hands and use words like labor dispute and welfare arrangement. Her father would laugh, challenging her to replace her hand with the gavel, unmindful of the streak of gravy trickling down the edge of his lips to dissolve in his fleshy double chin. Done with lunch, they would move to the living room, where they'd indulge in more arguments. Then Sunil would stretch back on the sofa for a power nap before returning to work at exactly 12:55 p.m., leaving his daughter pining for his return to satiate each other's hunger for that one last heated clash of ideas, all of which would leave Sunil too exhausted and ready for sleep.

Ma stood at the kitchen door and watched them. Her husband's charitable posturing annoyed her. If he were so concerned about the maid's education, why did he treat the girl like a benign ghost?

Ma hoped the strike would be called off. If she could sell some stocks, she would invest in that garden where she'd grow rows of buttercups and magnolias. Perhaps build a nursery and start a small business. Standing over the dining table, Ma was mulling over this and that when Geeta appeared with blood-stained bandages wrapped around both palms.

"Who will take me to the doctor?" she said.

"Didn't you help her?" Ma asked her daughter.

"I was about to," Meena said.

"I put the bandage on myself," Geeta said.

"So sorry, I was about to come to your room," Meena said.

"Insensitive brat," Ma said, her eyes fixed on Meena.

"You pushed her. I didn't," Meena said, prompting Sunil to look at Ma.

"You hit her again?" he said.

"It was an accident."

"Was it an accident?" Meena asked the maid.

"No," the maid said, startling everyone.

"How dare you." Ma turned to Geeta.

Sunil posed a questioning eye at his wife, as if he had grown tired of constantly listening to her drama, her mistreatment of the maid.

"I'm tired of living under a dark cloud in this house," Meena said.

"Find your own place then. I'm sure you won't have a problem sleeping around," Ma said.

"Watch your mouth," Sunil said to her. His veins got entangled on his forehead. He had never spoken to her that way, never raised his voice, but in that moment, Ma felt like all the regrets that had hardened into his veins could burst into an explosion when she least expected it, in the form of a seizure, a heart attack, just to punish her, as if that were his way of claiming his due.

Sunil stared at her, defied her to cross the line. When Ma regained her composure, the maid had already left.

"You father and daughter suffocate me," she said and left the room.

～

"Geeta, Geeta," Ma said, standing outside the one-room shed where the maid slept.

Bruno, the family dog, whined from his cage, reluctantly wagging his tail. But there was no sign of the maid. Ma opened the makeshift door, a rough plank of wood without a knob. The room was about the size of Ma's bathroom. In a corner she saw discarded taps, pipes, and a rusty power generator. A nylon rope nailed on opposite corners hung across the room from which dangled a few scraps of clothing, giving the place a dank odor. Ma realized she had never been inside this room before.

From the gatekeeper she found out that Geeta had walked toward the market.

Moments later, Ma was in her car, driving down the tree-lined street, when she saw Geeta walking by the side of the road. Ma slowed the car down and opened the passenger door, but Geeta kept walking, so Ma followed with a gentle release of the foot pedal. "Don't waste your time and mine. You need to go to the doctor," she said.

Smelling faintly of dried blood, Geeta sat next to Ma, looking physically smaller than she did in the morning.

Her uncle had brought her to Ma's house two years prior through the chauffeur's connection. The ten-year-old girl crouched on the floor by the kitchen door. She wore a long flounce skirt, and her oily hair was braided on two sides with ropelike patterns. She was thin and dark-skinned, with big eyes that hid a mischievous twinkle. At first, she looked at Ma curiously, then she suddenly smiled, exposing uneven teeth.

"You've picked her up from dirt," the uncle had said and left the girl at the mercy of Ma for a small amount. Ma had been relieved to find a child servant unburdened by cynicism after years of merry-go-rounds with servants, male and female, adept at mind games and thievery. Ma never discriminated on food, and the satisfaction with which Geeta ate basmati rice with chicken and organic vegetables everyday spoke of her appreciation. The thought of losing the maid's companionship bothered her.

Ma turned a corner from their quiet neighborhood into the busy market.

"If you hit me one more time, I'll leave," Geeta said.

"Sorry, now," Ma said, secretly smiling at where the girl could possibly go back to.

"I'll tell Meena dijju you look at her phone."

"Stop it, now. You don't make it easier either. You can be so mischievous."

"Send me to school then," Geeta said. "I'm already too old for first standard."

"You're never too old for school," Ma said after a long pause. She made up her mind. She knew she had to seize every opportunity to establish her authority in her own house.

"I won't let you down," the maid said. They made eye contact. Geeta's hair had come undone from its knot, hanging wildly about her face.

Like a child who had gone to sleep, dreaming of things that only children were capable of, to find herself all grown up, working as a maid the next morning.

Ma instinctively reached out to touch the girl's face. "You better not even think about letting me down," she said, and they drove away before the sky would soften with an orange tinge and the voices of crows would ring out from tall dark trees behind her house.

Acknowledgments

Thanks to all my professors, especially Robert Anthony Siegel and S. Shankar, whose insight and support lay the seeds of my writing life. Thanks to Samrat Upadhyay for being an inspiration and always responding to my emails with an attentive ear. Thank you, colleagues and friends, including Natasha Saje, Joseph Cardinale, Tom Gammarino, Snezana Zabic, and Abha Eli, for their generosity and feedback over the years. A special thanks to my agent Kanishka Gupta as well as Amish Raj Mulmi and Priya Sanyal at Writer's Side for their guidance and feedback. Thanks to all the wonderful people at Penguin Random House India and University of Wisconsin Press, especially Moutushi Mukherjee and Dennis Lloyd for sharing the joy and suffering in this process. Your insight helped these stories become their best selves. Thanks to my editors Jessica Smith and Saloni Mital, Thanks to Westminster University for your support and for funding various stages of research, and lastly, thanks to my ex-wife and friend Jessica Kafle for reading early drafts and being a good sounding board always, and my father, mother, brother and his family for their love and support; my father, especially, for being an excellent reader. And, of course, thanks to my son Tenzing for being the joy of my life.